SHERLOCK HOLMES
The Ultimate Satyr Collection

VOLUME 1

By

Pennie Mae Cartawick

Copyright

Contents

SHERLOCK HOLMES

The Mystery of the Poisoned Tomb

The first I heard of Holmes and I travelling to Egypt was when my friend laid out on the breakfast table amongst the tea and toast, a suitcase packed with my clothes. Now we were riding on horseback, the blistering heat bearing down on our faces. I constantly mopped my brow with a handkerchief and I was flabbergasted to see that Holmes was not affected at all! He tilted his head as if there was a gentle breeze and cheerfully told me, "Cheer up, old chap, you did prescribe me a holiday." "I meant a weekend break in the countryside, not in a sweltering desert!" "Cold, wet Yorkshire with the only intriguing thing being a case of sheep thievery." Holmes smiled to himself. "Aren't you excited? Egyptian artifacts are much more fascinating in their habitat rather than locked up in a dusty museum or private collection."

Our destination was an archaeological dig in the Valley of the Kings. There seemed to be more Americans and Britons in Egypt than there were Egyptians, the furor for unique and expensive artifacts had stormed through the upper classes. Those with money paid for professors and their eager students to trawl through the endless dunes of sand. The artifacts I had seen in the museum had been amazing, scarab brooches and jars with dog's head stoppers. "Almost there Watson Look, you can see them from here." I strained my eyes and saw the hunched figures of the Egyptian workers who had been hired to dig. As we drew closer I saw turbans and robes billow from their movements. There was one man who paced amongst them. His arms were crossed and he clasped a long strap of leather. I assumed he must have been the foreman. He watched us with an incalculable expression.

A small distance away a small tent had been set up. When we slowed to a stop and descended, a small sprightly man flung aside the curtains and strode out. His arms were spread wide in welcome, a fez clutched in each hand, and a third fez rested on his curly head of hair as he boomed out, "Welcome to Egypt!" And the American promptly placed a fez on each of our heads. "You look nothing like your brother Mr. Holmes," the man remarked. "Which I am glad for," Holmes replied as he shook the man's hand. "Watson, this is Benjamin Fairfax, a work colleague of Mycroft's." "Retired work colleague, actually, I couldn't hack it like Mycroft could. Now, come inside. Meet the wife."

Fairfax's wife was a dark haired beauty with a rosy cheeked complexion. She was sitting before a small table with tea and scones on it. The woman fanned herself with an oriental fan, her loose hair floating about her face from the intensity of her fanning as she watched the workers. The men outside could be seen through the curtains thin muslin. "Good morning," she smiled at us and resumed following their vague figures. "There's tea for you on the table," she murmured distractedly. "This is Jane." Fairfax leaned over and kissed her cheek. "It was she who suggested asking you to come here."

There were two seats set aside for us and we sat down. I took the two cups and gave one to Holmes whom promptly returned it back to the table. He then knocked off his hat and began fiddling with the tassel. "I was curious as to why you wanted my services."

Of course this wasn't a holiday; Holmes had found himself another case. The man was never going to relax. "I have a permit to dig at the Valley of the Kings," Fairfax began. "A windfall, this would most likely be where the Pharaohs were buried". "However, other digs in the area are being sabotaged" "How so?" I asked once I had finished my tea. Holmes attention was on the fez but I knew that he was focused entirely on the conversation. "I know these fellows. They wouldn't use fakes yet fake artifacts are appearing amongst genuine items. It's ruining the men's reputations and all of their other finds are being questioned - I do not want that happening to me. I want Holmes to find whoever's doing this."

"Would not the most obvious conclusion be that these men planted the fakes?" Holmes queried.

"No, I don't believe it. There's a saboteur".

"Very well, Mr. Fairfax I'll make certain that nothing spoils the legitimacy of your work."

It was then that one of the workers started shouting. The foreman, a tall, hulking man the complete opposite to Fairfax, entered the tent. "We've found something,

Madame, sir." The workers knelt around a hole in the ground. When the foreman approached, they scattered to reveal a passage leading further inwards. Fairfax rubbed his hands in anticipation. "You're my good luck charm Holmes! This could be the tomb to an undiscovered pharaoh!"

"Yes, how wonderful."

Holmes did not sound so cheerful. I carefully watched him as Fairfax and Jane led us down, to the stone wall that kept us from seeing what was inside. "Amun, have one of the workers knock this down. We are eager to see its contents," Fairfax ordered. Amun, the foreman, clapped his hands and told one of the men in the language what they should bring.

The man soon returned, he carried a sledgehammer and dragged it behind him. We stood aside and waited as he hauled it up with surprisingly strong hands and watched him brake down the wall. "Lanterns" Fairfax shouted and lit lanterns were brought down to us. He stepped over the debris and hurried into the tunnel without waiting for us, Holmes was the next person to enter and Jane hoisted up her skirt though not enough to reveal her ankles so that she too could climb over the shattered stone. "I was not the last person to follow them; the Egyptian man who carried the sledgehammer was close behind me". The man kept his head bowed, as though he did not want anyone to see his face, and I could hear him quietly whisper to himself. The words were fast, frantic and repetitive, like a prayer. If I was not already unnerved by having to walk through a cramped, almost dark tunnel then I certainly was then!

I could see Holmes running his fingers along the tunnel wall. I wondered what he was doing, feeling to see if anyone had been here before us. Another stone wall lay in our path, we pressed our backs to the walls to allow the worker to squeeze past and destroy it. The air tasted stale and there was a faint, almost sweet smell. It must have been Mrs. Fairfax's perfume; it now smelt too strong as we were no longer in an open space. I heard her gasp as she went inside and it was soon my turn to gape in amazement. There were hieroglyphics drawn on the roof of the tomb. Eyes and flat figures of men and women stared back at me.

Papyrus scrolls were stacked atop of one another in an imitation of a pyramid. I saw another jar with a dog's head topper. The tomb wasn't awash with relics but there was enough to interest anyone. I didn't recognize all of them, goodness knew what they had been used for in the past, and I turned to Holmes to ask him what he thought of it... He was behaving most peculiar. Holmes had scooped up some of the sand on the ground with his fez; it was only I who noticed his odd actions. He carried it under his arm, so that no one could see what it held, and resumed examining the Horus statue in front of him. I made a note to ask him later on what he was up to. However, I could see no sarcophagi.

"Whose tomb was this? Did a Pharaoh reside here Holmes?" Fairfax inquisitively said while examining a glittering bracelet.

"The Pharaohs were normally kept in another hidden chamber. And if you look to your right you will notice the hairline fracture in the wall, indicating that there is something hollow behind it".

Fairfax signaled for the worker to knock that down next when Holmes added, "I believe you have to alert the Department of Antiquities about a tomb's discovery before you attempt to search for a sarcophagus."

Fairfax appeared frustrated but he agreed not to pursue his search. He lifted his head to look at the hieroglyphics.

"What do you think they say?" He asked himself. "They say, do not enter, for Ra shall be displeased and darkness will enter your bodies'." We turned to see that it was the Egyptian man who had spoken. He was staring directly at Fairfax. "It is a curse for those who enter uninvited."

Afterwards we travelled down to the hotel that Mr. and Mrs. Fairfax and we were staying in. We dined on Kibbe, toasting our discovery with Fairfax's finest claret, and tried desperately hard not to think back on the worker's worrying translation."Ini is a superstitious man", Fairfax told us over his glass. "I would have been worried if he hadn't given us a doom laden prophecy." Jane laughed at his words. "Do not worry, doctor, detective," she said. "The only thing that can stop us now is the Department of Antiquities!"

When we retired to bed I knocked on Holmes door to see how he felt. A faint pain had been building up in my stomach since we had eaten, and I had felt light headed and bilious. "Enter Watson." Holmes was sitting before his microscope. He had carefully wrapped it up in tissue paper when he had packed it in England to ensure he could travel without it breaking. The fez, with only half of the sand he had taken in it, was next to him. "What are you doing?" I asked as I sat down on his bed. "Examining the sand from the tomb, Fairfax was quick to get inside and trample over the entire area; however, I believe this sample has been relatively untouched".

"You're suspicious of him?"

"I suspect he is trying to fool the Department of Antiquities. It was no coincidence that a tomb was suddenly 'discovered' after you and I had only just arrived." Even Holmes looked a little worse for wear. He was constantly clearing his throat, rather like a cat with hair stuck in its throat, and I could see sweat beading on the back of his neck. The heat was finally getting to him. I groaned while lying down, I felt too exhausted to get up. "Have you found anything?" I wasn't awake to hear Holmes' reply.

I woke up to find myself half sprawled on the bed and Holmes lying across the desk, the microscope shoved aside. My stomach no longer hurt and the flushed feeling had died down, however I still felt uneasy. It must have been something we had eaten. I had not noticed any vials in Holmes' suitcase, so I doubted he had taken anything to cause his own lethargy. "Holmes!" I shook him and my friend rubbed at his eyes. "Ah good morning John, if we do not hurry then we shall miss the unveiling of the sarcophagus." He leapt up, feeling much better than I did, and chased me into my own room so that I could get changed.

There was a large crowd who had come to see the tomb. Holmes and I made our way through. I noticed Ini intently watching us. Mr. and Mrs. Fairfax were standing in the tunnel with someone from the Department of Antiquities.

They had been waiting for us. The five of us made our way through the tunnel and back to the tomb. I couldn't wait to see if there really was a Pharaoh in the next room. There was a body on the ground. It was Amun. He lay by the feet of the Horus statue and already the body smelt as foul as a week old corpse. His hands clutched handfuls of his torn out hair. He had vomited several times. The eyes were wide and made him look as if he was in shock. Jane Fairfax swooned into her husband's arms, crying out that the curse had taken Amun from them. Fairfax seemed as if he could not comprehend the scene before him. The antiquities man let out a horrified moan. Holmes had crossed his arms in quiet contemplation.

The man from the Department of Antiquities had run out of the tomb to alert the authorities. Within minutes Holmes was acquainting himself with the corpse. "Be careful, Mr. Holmes!" Jane Fairfax called out as her senses returned. "You shouldn't touch him... what if he is contagious?" "Then we might already have it if it is airborne." Holmes replied, though he did pull on a pair of riding gloves from his pocket. "Watson." At the sound of my name I came over to his side. The papyrus scrolls had been disturbed, the little pyramid had toppled. Other things had fallen, bracelets, brooches, I was careful not to accidentally step on them. Holmes lifted Amun's left hand and examined the fingers. I could see that the nails were discolored. There was a faint, red stain on his wrist, Holmes sniffed it. "Claret," he muttered to himself.

My friend's eyes had narrowed, his thin, bloodless lips moved soundlessly as he noted everything I could not see. I knew that he no longer noticed the Fairfaxes or myself, his mind's eye saw only the evidence. He was opening Amun's tightly closed fist when I heard footsteps hurrying towards the tomb. "Holmes," I hissed, his eyes focused on me, before I could see what he had found in Amun's hand he had pocketed it. "The police here might not be as understanding as detective Lestrade is."

He got up and moved away from the body, as did I, just as the police came storming inside. As the police ushered us out of the tomb I heard a faint murmur amongst the workers, Arabic and Egyptian words weaving through the masses, and there was a name interwoven with them; Ini. The man was no longer in the area. "That man - Ini - Holmes, he isn't here." "I know," Holmes said. "Question the workers. Ini either knows something we do not and he is implicated somehow or he has just been accused of the murder and carted away."

It was the latter. Ini had been seen late last night entering the tomb and then running back out. Several rumors had already emerged; that Ini had called down the curse of Ra upon Amun; Ini had planned to rob the tomb and Amun had come across him; Amun and Ini had argued over something and a dozen other tales. However, there was a general agreement amongst the workers that Amun had got his comeuppance. The leather strap he had carried was used often on young or old backs. He seemed to take pleasure in meting out punishment. Amun was not missed.

Ini had been taken in for questioning and Holmes and I were waiting for our chance to see him. "Discolored fingernails, hair loss and vomiting," I mused as Holmes paced. "If only I could get my hands on the coroner's report. We'd know for certain if it was arsenic if white powder is found in Amun's stomach." "And if the medical examiner finds nothing, then it will be blamed on the curse... all except by the police, who will still suspect Ini either way." Holmes paused. "Had he killed Amun in a fit of rage or panic, it would have been through violence rather than poison... and there is one definitive reason why Amun was poisoned in the tomb."

"You know, Holmes," I began. "We too were unwell when we had returned from the tomb, though it did not lead to our deaths." "How else is a curse considered a curse unless it affects everyone who has supposedly come into contact with it?" He ran a hand through his hair and then pulled one of the hairs out. He held it to his eye. "Doctor, when we return to the hotel I would be in your debt if you could somehow acquire hair from each Fairfax."

"Holmes?"

"I believe enough time has passed for any arsenic to have revealed its presence."

When Ini was released back into his cell we were taken to him, after Holmes had bargained with the guard. At our arrival Ini looked up at us despondently, the man's hands were shackled together and his foot was badly cut. No one had seen fit to bandage it and I could do nothing with the cell door locked. "Ini, come over here," I told him and the man rose, limping towards us. "Now sit down and stick your foot through the bars." He did as I asked and I knelt. I tore a strip from my shirt. It was a poor substitute, however it would have to do for now. I was about to wrap it around Ini's foot when Holmes stopped me. "A moment Watson" He too knelt and unearthed a pair of tweezers from the depths of his, often untidy, pockets. "Don't mind me Ini," he remarked cheerfully, "Just gathering some evidence." From the cut he pulled out a thin sliver of glass which I hadn't even noticed. "Carry on, doctor." I resumed bandaging Ini's wound. Once I had finished, Ini returned to sitting on the cell bench and Holmes quietly questioned him.

"Did you go to the tomb to rob it?"

"No, I did not!" Ini slammed his fist on the bench. "I am not a common thief!"

"Then what are you?"

"I am a protector of my people's heritage."

"The saboteur" Holmes recalled.

"The English and Americans bring with them money but they take priceless relics - to be locked away in foreign museums and sold on the black market - when they should stay in Egypt. What would you do if I was to come to your country, steal one of your relics, and never bring it back?"

"What did you do exactly?"

"I made fakes of the things I had seen while working on digs, then swapped the real relic for the fake so that the rich men's permits would be taken from them."

"And where did you put the artifacts?"

"... I hid them in an abandoned tomb."

"That sounds rather like a private collection," Holmes suggested.

"I am hiding them!" The man snapped. "So that one day, when the Department of Antiquities is no longer in the richest man's pocket, Egypt may celebrate its treasures."

"Why are you telling us this?" I queried. "Surely the police will suggest you poisoned Amun because he discovered what you were about to do?"

"I am not a murderer... and I know your friend is a detective. Will he help me?" "Of course, I will," Holmes said. "But first you must describe to me what you saw in the tomb last night." Ini nodded and drew in a breath. "I had a fake necklace I was going to place in the tomb. I snuck inside... it was then that I saw Amun. He was on the ground,

17

still, dead; I was only in there for a few moments. I ran out and stepped on some glass and that was how I cut my foot... wouldn't stop bleeding, cursed thing."

There had been no broken glass in the tomb when we had been in there. "Did you see anyone?"

"No only Amun."

"Thank you Ini. Now, all I need is the location of where you hid the artifacts."

I returned to the hotel, Holmes had gone off on his horse to where Ini's tomb was. My task was to get a hair sample from Mr. and Mrs. Fairfax, though it would not be a simple task. Holmes would need a chunk of hair, not the one strand as I had earlier believed. Fairfax was currently helping the police while his wife was in their hotel room. I knocked and opened the door when she called for me to enter. "Hello, doctor." She was sitting in front of her dresser mirror, brushing her hair with quick, sharp jerks. Jane placed the brush down and pressed her fingers to her forehead, eyes shut tight. "Goodness, I was hoping this headache would go but it's been bothering me since last night." "Jane," I began. "Holmes suspects arsenic poisoning. He said he could detect arsenic through a hair sample... if you wouldn't mind?"

"A hair sample?" ... Of course not doctor, not if it will help Mr. Holmes find out what has happened. There's some scissors over there." I picked up the scissors and very gently snipped a small amount of hair at the root. In the palm of my hand the hair appeared limp, rather like grass plucked out of the ground. Mr. Fairfax strode into the room, his voice was panicked, "Jane, the police have said they've discovered arsenic in Amun's stomach!" His eyes fell on me. "Think of it, we might all have been poisoned!" "Hush, Benjamin," Jane said soothingly. She reached out and petted his hand, reminding me of a young girl and an overanxious dog. "Surely this is better than believing that the God Ra might have cursed us." "I guess so..." "Mr. Holmes had already found out about the arsenic dear, he wants some of our hair to see if we too were targeted." "Our hair but surely..." "I've already given the good doctor here a sample."

Mr. Fairfax took the scissors from me and reluctantly cut off a curl. It was then that Holmes arrived. His cheeks were flushed from his ride and he dusted sand off of his trousers. He eyed the curl and locks of dark hair and took them from me. "Ah splendid, I shall examine them posthaste."

I waited in Holmes' room, sitting on his bed as I had done last night, while he peered through his microscope at the hair samples. I had no idea what he was thinking; all I saw was the long curve of his hunched back.

"I thought it took a week for hair to grow, it has only been an evening since our suspected poisoning."

"That was simply a ruse. What I really wanted was Mr. Fairfax's hair."

Holmes fell silent, entirely engrossed with the single curl. I opened up my journal, planning on doing something productive if Holmes was going to ignore me for the rest of the night - "A-hah, I was right!" However, Holmes did not clarify what exactly he was right about.

The next morning Holmes was banging on the Fairfax's door, I had watched him all night smoking his pipe and tapping his foot on the ground. He'd been piecing everything together. He would have liked to have gone to the Fairfax's room in the middle of the night but I had dissuaded him from it, if they did not like what he said then they could simply throw us out for bothering them at an indecent hour.

The only person in the room was Jane. In her hand was a letter opener and before her was a flurry of correspondence. Mrs. Fairfax cleanly sliced the letter open and greeted us as we came inside. A cup of tea quietly cooled on the dresser table next to her empty cup. "I was expecting my husband for morning tea but he seems to have wandered off," she laughed. "Typical! Perhaps you can keep me company while I wait for him?"

"Of course" I sat down in a chair, however Holmes remained standing.

"Thank goodness it isn't a curse," Jane told us with a smile, glancing momentarily at the contents of her letter and then moving onto the next one. "Though I am worrying about my hair falling out from the arsenic; that won't happen, will it, doctor?" "No, dear," I said. "We were only given minor doses."

"Which you intended Mrs. Fairfax," Holmes abruptly announced. Mrs. Fairfax put down the letter, her smile still in place. "Whatever could you be speaking of Mr. Holmes?"

"Deceit, forging a tomb, the cold, calculated murders of your lover and husband."

She blinked in confusion and I turned to look at Holmes. "What's this about Holmes?" I asked.

"All of the items inside the tomb that was discovered came from different digs."

"You cannot mean -?"

"Yes, the artifacts Ini stole. I suspect Amun followed him one day and found his hiding place, Ini had no idea his horde was missing until I returned to his cell and told him yesterday. Your dig did unearth a tomb, however it was ransacked. Fairfax was desperate for fame; Mycroft was quick to warn me that Fairfax couldn't stand not being seen as important. When Amun, your lover, told you what Ini had, your husband, Amun and you planned to fake a tomb."

"Then why would I invite you here?" Mrs. Fairfax

countered. "And Amun was most certainly not my lover!"

"I suppose your reasoning was that if you could fool me then you could fool anyone. You were the one in control of this, Amun deferred to you at the dig... and the lock of hair that was found clasped in his hand, amongst his own of course, was a lock of your own hair that you must have gifted him." That was what Holmes had found in Amun's hand!

Mrs. Fairfax drummed her fingers on the table. She was not impressed. "This is all just speculation, that tomb is genuine."

"Then why is it I found traces of yourself, Amun and your husband in a sample of sand from the tomb that should not be there."

"You were mistaken, Benjamin entered before you did, and you could not have possibly seen every step he made."

"No, however Amun did not enter the tomb with us. You also forgot to reapply your perfume, you were wearing it the first time you entered the tomb but not when you were down there with us."

She said nothing in reply. Her smile had been replaced with a cool, uncaring expression.

"It was agreed that you would pretend there was a curse and dose yourself and us with mild arsenic, however, Amun was not so lucky. You no longer required him, and secrets are better kept when one of them can no longer speak. You arranged to meet with him in the tomb and offered him some claret, with an added kick to it." Holmes revealed the sliver of glass he had pulled from Ini's foot. "Amun dropped the glass and before you could clean it up Ini stumbled upon you, you hid and once Ini had left, you swept away the glass and went back to the hotel leaving Amun to fall into a coma and die. But not before he pulled out your lock of hair. The only thing I do not know is whether or not he was mourning the failed relationship, or if he was pointing us to his murderess."

"Why..." She swallowed. "If this was true then why would I want to kill my husband?"

"Benjamin wanted fame; you wanted his money or simply him out of the way. There are only two people who have received high dosages of arsenic, Amun and Benjamin Fairfax. Both were steadily poisoned over a time period of several months... and I suspect Fairfax's last, lethal dose is in that cup of tea. It is a good thing Watson and I saw him earlier today, he soon crumbled and revealed all that he knew."

Mrs. Fairfax bowed her head and I thought she was going to cry when she sprung out of her chair and went for Holmes with the letter opener! Holmes held her back but she was wild with rage, her face bright red and her teeth crept in to view like a wild animal. "That stupid, insipid, spoilt fool!"

She snarled. "How dare - how dare he betray me! How dare you deceive me" I rushed up and pulled her arms behind her back, she struggled violently against me. She kicked and screamed. And the letter opener fell from her hand.

"You said that there was one definitive reason why Amun had been poisoned in the tomb," I told Holmes on the boat back to England. "What did you mean?"

"Mrs. Fairfax could not move Amun by herself; she had to do it in the tomb."

"Ah," I paused and I couldn't help but remark to my friend, "In all honesty Holmes, I much prefer 'cold, wet Yorkshire' to Egypt!"

SHERLOCK HOLMES

The Mystery of the Faceless Bride

It was a rather calm evening when Holmes and I heard hurried footsteps coming up Mrs. Hudson's stairs. We had only just arrived from our night out at the theatre, Holmes had spent the entire time announcing every hole in the plot and every twist to an audience who were steadily losing their patience, and we had quickly vacated before Holmes could utter the killer's name and the fact that they had an obsession with cats.

Holmes had been sitting in his armchair, still wearing his evening wear and smoking, and I had been changing into my nightclothes in the other room when the aforementioned footsteps occurred and there was a terrific banging noise upon the door. I half expected it to smash open and a brute of a man fall inside! I ran back into the sitting room, putting on my dressing gown, and asked Holmes what the blazes was going on.

Holmes paused and blew out a ring of smoke. "You shouldn't have bothered changing, dear chap. Open the door now, would you?"

I tightened my belt and hesitantly went to the door. I Shuddered from the pounding it was receiving and I would not have been surprised if Mrs. Hudson had soon appeared, brandishing a pot and broom. When I opened the door I thought it might have been another ruffian after Holmes, a relative of someone he had put away with his deductions, but it was a young woman who was half my size. Her bruised knuckles were raised to bang the door, her tongue kept on creeping out to lick away the blood beading on her lip. She was in a frightful state. One side of her face had swelled up and I doubted she could see out of her right eye, her clothes were torn and muddied. The woman should have been weeping yet she appeared to be frantic with rage.

"Where is he?" She painfully slurred. "Where's Mr. Sherlock Holmes? I need him." I ushered her inside and made to direct her to a chair but she bared her rotten teeth at me. She stood in front of Holmes with dark, dried blood streaked through her light red hair and she had her arms wrapped around her sides.

"I am right here, Mercy," Holmes answered her, continuing on as she gaped. "I noticed you staggering after us the moment Doctor Watson and I left the cab."

"Holmes!" I admonished him as I picked up a clean rag and alcohol. "We could have helped her, not left her to drag herself here!"

"She wouldn't have accepted the help." Holmes turned his head to look at me and answered my curious expression, completely ignoring Mercy. "This is Mercy Doolan, a matchstick girl. The youngest child from the Doolan family with five brothers; I imagine she has come to us regarding one of them." I watched as Mercy's anger quickly descended into disbelief.

"How did you find that out?"

"Does your jaw hurt, Mercy?" Holmes began. "It must be taking all of your energy to speak. Rotten teeth are normally the outcome of poor hygiene, however combined with the purloined matches you have sticking out of your pocket -" At his words Mercy's fingers pushed the matches until they were hidden away. "- then it is obvious to assume you work in a match factory. "For several years considering the deterioration of your teeth and jaw from the phosphorus fumes:"

"And my name"

"One of your brothers sells newspapers here at Baker Street. I have noticed you meeting him, most likely to give him the matches to sell, and street sellers are not known to be quiet." Holmes laughed to himself. "There was no need for deductions in that regard; I even know when your mother's next baby is due."

It was then that Mercy finally gave in to her body's demands for rest. I caught her as she stumbled and forced her into the chair that I normally sat in opposite Holmes.

"You're all the same," she tiredly murmured, "you posh boys, sneering at us because we were born in the wrong house. If you're really as clever as the papers say you are, figure out what's happened to me."

"Well, a fight of some sort, though I will leave Watson to

deduce your injuries." My fingers ran through her bloodied hair and I found the source. There was a gash on the side of her head that had healed not that long ago. I poured some alcohol on my cloth and dabbed at it, she wriggled and tightly clenched her hands in discomfort.

"She's been hit hard, Holmes," I said in disbelief, the young woman certainly had a tongue on her but that didn't warrant a beating. "With a weapon of some sort;"

"A cricket bat," Mercy answered. "Will I need stitches doctor? Will I have to pay for them?"

"No, to both of those questions;" I shook my head. "I'm not about to charge you when you look like you've crawled out of a grave."

"More like punched her way out of a grave considering the state of her hands," Holmes added. "Now, do stop fussing over her, Watson. I'm sure Miss Doolan would prefer us to get started on her case... if she is willing to tell us about it rather than continuously be in a bad humor."

Holmes leaned forward and I noticed Mercy shifting uneasily. At that moment Holmes resembled the elongated shadow of a cat that was waiting for a mouse to appear. Although the young woman had arrived beaten and in desperate need of our help; there was nothing interesting about a fight, the police could run after attackers. Holmes wanted an intrigue.

"Johnny's been working really hard to better himself," Mercy told us as she pressed the bottle against her face. "He's been going to night classes with money he's saved up and trying to catch the eye of someone who would sponsor him."

"Did he find someone?" I asked.

Mercy nodded. "The old gent Johnny's been working for in the stables picked him up, like some charity case. He said he liked the sight of a determined lad, as his own were lazy and spoilt, and that he would be willing to pay for his schooling. Johnny's been going to the college for a year now. Ma and pa, they were pleased at first, they thought Johnny would be the making of this family and then we wouldn't have to go to the factories." She wouldn't look either of us in the eye.

"Was it you Mercy, rather than your mother and father, who were upset about Johnny's sudden prospects?" Holmes wondered, his keen, dark eyes were too intense for the young woman, as it was for many people, she looked at me instead.

"Johnny was happy there but he didn't realize it was changing him. Whenever he came off the train I could see it in his eyes. He was starting to think that we were too common for him! I couldn't believe it when he changed his name to 'Jonathan' and started to put on a posh voice. It made me so angry that I told him not to bother coming again, that he could stay with his pals if he thought they were better than us... but he still sent letters, up until last week."

"And you decided to search for him."

"I got on the train and travelled down to the college. I tried one of the teachers but they thought I was after cleaning work, wouldn't even speak to me, so I asked the students. A lot of them laughed at me and said that no brother with a voice like mine would study alongside them. I got mad, started shouting at them... and was chased off by one of groundskeepers." Mercy sighed to herself. "I'd given up; I was going back to London when a group of them came up to me. They said they knew where Johnny was, and that they could show me."

"And did you follow them?"

"Of course I did! What else could I do? They took me to a churchyard. There were so many graves around us, and I asked them to tell me where he was. They said the bride had got him..."

"Bride" Holmes asked curiously.

"I didn't know what they meant. I told them not to be silly

and to tell the truth... they laughed at me. I told them off and said I'd see them in hell. There was one; I think he was the leader, who kept on rubbing his neck for some reason. I couldn't help but notice because he did it so often. He said that I'd be with my brother soon enough, that the bride could have me next - and then he hit me! I fought them until I couldn't stand up anymore. I fainted."

This was simply too monstrous, goodness knew what those boys had done to her. I poured her a glass of brandy and she carefully sipped it. "When I woke up someone had made off with my coat and there were scratches on my arms. Like an animal had got at me. I stumbled back to the station and got the last train home, then; I ended up here."

Holmes leaned back and digested what he had heard. The mouse had appeared from its hole and enticed the cat. I knew that look in his face. The corners of his lips twitched as his mind raced through all the possibilities of what could have happened to Mercy's brother. Mercy didn't matter anymore; all he wanted to do now was race off to the college and meet this mysterious bride.

"Holmes," I quietly reminded him of the matter at hand. "Should we not ensure that Miss Doolan returns home safely, and then plan what we will do next?"

He waved his hand nonchalantly. "I will pay for her cab fare home if you must insist upon it, Doctor."

"Really" Mercy's face brightened. "I can come back tomorrow with some money I've put aside to pay you to look for Johnny."

"Your matchsticks will do nicely for payment, Miss Doolan. I will require nothing else."

With a dumbfounded expression Mercy pulled out her matches and handed them to Holmes, who replenished his pipe with tobacco and lit it. As he puffed away he smiled to himself. "I will find your brother and lift the veil off of this bride!"

The next day Holmes and I were on the train to Berkshire. I was flicking through today's Times while he was resting next to me. His coat was pulled up to his neck and his hat was pushed down low. He did not fool me. Whenever someone new came into the compartment his eyes would open slightly and a muffled voice would issue, describing where they had come from and where their final destination would be. A lean looking country curate, a newly widowed woman and a portly businessman off on a seaside jaunt with his mistress had walked straight back out of the compartment at the sound of his voice.

When we disembarked; Holmes stretched and remarked upon what a peaceful train journey it had been. We hired a pony and trap from the station to take us to the college. In the distance I saw the college's many arches and was faintly reminded of the simple but noble symmetry of a church. Holmes had no time for the architecture, instead he pointed out a chapel as we went past, remarking that Mercy had most likely been led there and attacked. I had expected Holmes to approach one of the teachers or the headmaster in regards to the boy's disappearance; however once we had left the trap Holmes loitered around the Colleges front gates. We watched as students filed in and out. It was only when a group of them passed that Holmes suddenly barked out, "You, boy! Come here!" A few looked at us peculiarly but one rather timid boy broke away from the group.

"Yes, sir"

"What's all this nonsense I've been hearing in my classroom" Holmes hands went behind his back and he tilted his head ever so slightly so that only his eyes were looking down at the boy. "Bout a bride"

"You mean the faceless bride, sir?"

"Is there any other brides?"

"N-No," the boy stammered. "Mr. Danforth would beat us if we said there was another bride.

"Really, Why"

"Because he doesn't like us telling tales"

"Fine, tell me about this 'faceless bride'."

"It was the Cross and Knife club that started it. About a year ago they went down to the chapel and when they came back they said they'd seen a woman climb out of a grave. She was dressed in her bridal dress and carrying dead roses. When she approached them, she rose up her veil and there was no face underneath, only a gaping mouth that wanted to kiss them." The boy rubbed at his mouth as though he could feel the kiss of this creature. "They said they locked her up in the vaults of the chapel but nobody believes them, only..."

"Yes, what is it?" I gently asked.

"Three of the other students have gone missing since then. Whenever the club meets in the chapel for an initiation, the initiate vanishes."

At Holmes' dismissal; the boy ran back to his friends. Holmes rubbed his hands together and faced me with a mischievous shine in his eyes. "I believe a midnight prayer is in order, Watson."

When night descended Holmes and I made our way to the chapel carrying a lantern and pistol. On my first sighting of it earlier I had supposed that it was still in use, however as we drew nearer I noticed debris on the ground. I could not help but feel unnerved at how empty and abandoned it appeared to be. It would not be such a stretch to assume a ghost resided here.

"Watson, look!" Holmes hissed. Beyond one of the broken chapel windows we could see lights and hear the sound of laughter. We stealthily entered. There was a fight taking place. The pews, what was left of the gutted remains of the building, were pushed aside. In the middle of the room was a rabble of college students. They jeered and whooped as two young men boxed with naked, bloodied knuckles. Their panting breath echoed alongside the smack of fist hitting flesh. Not only was the Cross and Knife club ghost hunters, they had taken the sport of boxing to its most brutal heights. I was faintly reminded of a dog fight, with a pit bull versus a lapdog. It was a young boy, probably in his first year of college, against the eldest boy in the group. It was obvious who the victor would be.

Holmes had cupped his hand around the lantern's flame. He was entirely focused on the dynamics of the group, watching and deciphering who was the most powerful, who would be the ringleader. I followed Holmes' line of sight and saw a youth who wore a scarf emblazoned with the college's colors. Every few moments he would make a coughing motion and press his fingers to his jugular. The students were too engrossed in their game to pay any attention to their surroundings but I noticed a scuttling sound and it sounded too large for a rat. Holmes' eyes moved in the direction of the sound and indicated for me to go investigate. With my pistol in hand, I quietly made my way to the steps leading further into the chapel. The lights coming from the boys' candles soon drifted away, leaving me in semi-darkness. I pressed my hand against the wall to anchor myself and my hand came away wet with condensation. Wiping my palm onto my Jacket, I realized that these steps most likely led to the vaults, where the bride would be. I shook my head to chase off thoughts of a faceless bride removing her veil. It was then that I heard the brides nails upon the stone wall, Scratching, drawing closer and closer. When I turned... would it be a ghost or person I would face?

The bride carried no decaying roses but her bridal dress was torn and burnt. Her bare legs, starved needle points, staggered disjointedly. The veil hung low over her face. I had my pistol, however I could not shoot. If it was a ghost the bullet would surely pass through, if it was flesh then I would be shooting dead a woman. Her hands, the fingernails long and cracked, lifted up the veil. Her face! Even in the darkness I could see its ruin. The eyes had been snatched from its sockets, the nose sunken in; all that was left was the mouth. Thin, melted lips parted to reveal brown chipped teeth. A wheezing, gasping groan issued and once more she raised her hands, intent on strangling me! "Stay away-" I had begun to say but then she too spoke."...

Help me. Please." The words were hoarse, fainter than a whisper yet to my ears louder than a scream. This was no creature to be feared but to be pitied.

"Watson, come here, quickly!" Startled, the bride pushed past me and away before I could stop her. Holmes appeared at the top of the steps with the lantern held above his head. For a moment, with the lantern's light creating intense shadows, Holmes' face looked even gaunter than it usually did, his eyes black and empty. I shuddered, mind flashing back to the bride's tortured face.

"Holmes, the bride... I..."

"You saw it?"

I nodded and pointed behind me, deep into the vaults. "She was here only moments before. You frightened her off and she went down there."

"A runaway bride, eh" He murmured to himself. "She can wait."

"Why, what's wrong, Holmes?"

"It seems these boys have found an even stronger opponent to fight with."

Back in the chamber the boxing match had been broken up and another had started. The youth wearing the scarf now stood in the middle of the room and he was being accosted by a much older man. He had his arm around the boy's throat and as his captive struggled desperately against him the man roared at him, "I should have known this was your doing Shaw! Ragging with first years, and gambling, bringing shame to the school name; earning every single boy here a lashing for your stupidity." The man released Shaw and the boy stumbled forward. The group loitered awkwardly and was dismissed. They filed out of the chapel and back towards the college. Shaw was about to leave when a long, thin hand grasped his scarf.

"Boy," Holmes said as he pulled away the scarf to reveal the deep welts around Shaw's neck. "I think it's about time you acquainted us with the truth."

"I don't know what you're talking about sir," Shaw replied, then he turned to the man he had been fighting with. "It was only a little sporting fun Mr. Danforth."

"Now, you look like the sort of chap who enjoys kicking dogs or watching a fight rather than actually being involved in one... yet it appears someone has attempted to strangle you," Holmes countered.

"Look here," Mr. Danforth interjected as he stepped in-between Holmes and Shaw. "I'm this boy's teacher, if anyone's going to give him the lashing he deserves it shall be me."

"Yes, I had noticed you were a teacher from the chalk on your lapel."

Holmes released Shaw's scarf and proceeded to shake the man's hand. "... ah, and I see that you are the missing groom."

"What?" I asked with astonishment. "Holmes, you cannot surely mean-"

"Yes, Watson; on this man's ring finger there is a deep impression from a too tight ring. Had you been a widower Mr. Danforth, you would have kept the ring on or even replaced it with a new one once you had remarried. However this mark bears the familiar sign of a newly abandoned fiancée who has awaited their partner's return and then thrown the ring away in a pique of despair. Tell me sir; has it been a year since the future Mrs. Danforth was to be your bride?"

I could see that Holmes had wounded the teacher greatly. The man clenched his teeth and I was certain he was going to swing for him. "Shaw, get back to the college." Shaw sharply hurried off and it was Holmes, I, and Mr. Danforth who remained behind.

"How dare you bring that up in front of one of my boys," Danforth began and Holmes raised his hand in a soothing gesture.

"I am sure they already know. Young college boys are worse than women in that respect. It was them who started the rumor about a ghost bride".

"That blasted rumor, my classroom is awash with it."

"It is also true."

"Preposterous!" "My friend here, Doctor Watson, encountered her moments before."

"It's all true," I said. "She lifted up her veil and her face was horribly disfigured."

The teacher sat down in one of the pews and shook his head. He still did not believe us. Holmes leaned over him. "Has it been a year since your fiancée left?"

"Yes, a year since Anna left, on our wedding day no less!"

"Did you see her leave?"

"No, I... when she didn't arrive at the church I locked myself away in my rooms for several days." Holmes halfheartedly patted the man's shoulder and returned to my side, eager to resume the case. I saw Danforth bury his face into his hands.

"I believe it is time for us to go down to the vaults and reveal the truth behind this bridal rumor."

The lantern's light made the stairway seem less threatening

than before. Mr. Danforth was still bemoaning his luck upstairs as Holmes and I finally investigated the vaults. Holmes walked in front and lit the way while I could not stop myself from looking over my shoulder. There was only one vault we could enter, the others had caved in, and inside was a mass of items. An old, threadbare coat was in the corner, food was scattered across the stone coffin in the middle of the vault. Attached to one wall was a pair of chains and Holmes turned the shackles over in his hands. "Someone has used these recently Watson, there's blood on one of them." It was at that moment that a low groan sounded. I had thought the awful groaning noises meant the approach of the bride; however Holmes bounded over to the coat and threw it off with a flourish. There lay a young man who wore the college uniform. His skin was sickly and pale yet when I felt his forehead he was feverish. His light red hair was matted with sweat. As I checked him over Holmes busied himself with examining the coat. "He's suffering from a head wound," I said, lifting the man's head up slightly and pulling up his eyelids. "Possibly concussed;" Holmes dived into the coat pockets and pulled up the collar, removing a hair.

"A-hah" He announced triumphantly. "Match sticks and long red hair. I believe we have discovered where Mercy's coat vanished to." I could not fault him for his enthusiasm; however it was hard not to feel exasperated at his lack of concern over those who were not at that moment important to the case. I gently tapped the dazed young man's cheek in an attempt to rouse him. His eyes fluttered, "Johnny?" I said, guessing that this was who we were looking for. "Johnny, we've been sent by your sister to find you."

"Sister..? Mercy..?"

He weakly croaked. "Yes, we're going to carry you out now."

"No - wait!" He choked on his own exclamation. "There's a woman... down here. She helped me."

"How did you end up here?" I asked, for although I had a suspicion that Holmes had already figured it out, I had no idea of what had transpired. "We were going through my initiation into the Cross and Knife club." Johnny swallowed and his voice became a little clearer. "They locked me down here... That's when I found her... couldn't believe what I saw. When they let me out I said I was going to the headmaster. David... David Shaw... he hit me over the head with something and I woke up here."

"And where is the bride now Johnny?" Johnny wouldn't answer.

"She's right over there Watson," Holmes said as he indicated to the coffin. "She's been listening to us this entire time."

From her hiding place behind the coffin the bride revealed herself to us. Her head turned this way and that, searching.

"Anna." Holmes slowly came up to her.

"We've come to help you," I called out to her. The bride backed away from my friend and hunched in on herself. "Show me your hands." Anna held out her hands and I could see from where I kneeled, the bleeding welts on her wrists. "Did you try to throttle Shaw with the chain of your shackles a few nights back Anna?" Holmes continued his voice low and almost rhythmic. "I wouldn't hold it against you if you did." She nodded and Holmes moved until he was close enough to touch her. "Would you lift up your veil for me?"

Anna lifted her veil and Holmes held up the lantern so that it illuminated the ravages of her face. Her eyes were not gone but the skin of her eyelids had fused together, rendering her blind, and most of her flesh had melted like candle wax. She had been horrifically burned.

"Anna!" Danforth stood in the vault's entrance, he rushed over to her. "Oh, Anna"

"She's been down here for a year Danforth," Holmes told him "Held captive by your students."

"No, it can't be true!"

"They said..." Anna whispered. "That you did not look for me. I –"

Danforth could say nothing; by his own admission he had thought she had betrayed him. His expression became twisted with guilt. "I am here now Anna."

A few days later, when Johnny had recovered enough to travel, we took the first train home to London. Holmes constantly smoked his pipe and would not open the window, I was writing these very words in my journal and Johnny was staring out of the window. "Many a marriage has been formed through guilt," Holmes mumbled against the stem of his pipe. "Anna's and Danforth's will not be the last."

"How did it happen?" I asked. "Anna was going to be married yet a year later she's discovered burnt and imprisoned."

"Shaw told me that it had been a prank," Johnny gloomily answered. "That they'd make her miss her wedding and that Mr. Danforth would think he'd been jilted. They'd locked her up with a gas lamp but then there was a sudden explosion... it had exploded in her face. They were frightened they'd get into trouble so they kept her down there. As Shaw's guard dog, scaring students he didn't like back into their mother's arms!" He said with disgust.

Mercy Doolan was waiting for her brother at the station. "Johnny!" Mercy cried out and tightly embraced her brother. "Oh, you fool!" She hit him, and then she crumpled into his waiting arms. "I'm glad to see you too, Mercy."

As I watched the pair walk away and vanish into the crowd I turned to Holmes. "What do you suppose will happen to Shaw and the other boys? Will they be arrested?" Holmes took out his pocket watch and twisted the hands absentmindedly. "Holmes?" He put it away with a sigh and looked at me.

"Their fathers' money will most likely keep them out of prison; after all it was Shaw who imprisoned Anna. I knew that Shaw would escape into the night when he realized we had stumbled across his game."

"You could have said we could have stopped him from escaping."

"No," Holmes told me. "Shaw can only run for so long. Danforth will be in hot pursuit and don't forget... Danforth promised Shaw a lashing the next time he saw him."

SHERLOCK HOLMES

The Case of the Cracked Mirror

I had just managed to convince Holmes to take a sabbatical in a country cottage, overlooking calming rural countryside which had hares running across it rather than cases. When I arrived at 221B Baker Street I caught him half out the door with his suitcase in his hand.

"You're keen!" I greeted him cheerfully.

"Yes, I am," my friend replied, his normally sallow cheeks were glowing.

"See," I said knowingly. "Time off in the countryside will do you a world of good."

"Whatever are you talking about, dear chap?"

"The holiday of course" A familiar sense of unease settled in my stomach. "The one you agreed to go on yesterday.

Holmes laughed. "I don't know anything about that but I am off to France. Care to join me, Watson?"

The hansom we were now in was taking us to the Paris Opera house. Alongside the steady clop of the horses' hooves I listened to Holmes' excuse.

"I was contacted only this morning by the Comte Philippe de Chagny, the head of a rather eminent French family. His younger brother, Raoul, has got himself involved with a chorus girl from the opera house."

"Is that so unusual?" I asked. "Surely this is a domestic matter if Philippe de Chagny does not agree with his brother's love affairs?"

"The chorus girl has gone missing," my friend replied. "And Raoul has been searching for her without rest. Philippe is afraid of the scandal that will arise if the papers catch a hold of the fact that she is involved with a Chagny."

"Heavens, what do you suppose has happened to the girl?"

"I have heard rumors that the opera ghost stole away Christine Daae."

He turned his head and I saw him scrutinize the Paris Opera house as it came into view. A beautiful building, my eye was particularly drawn to the gilt copper L'Harmonie, a sculpture of a group of angels. When we entered, the first person we saw was Viscount Raoul de Chagny. The man was frantically pacing as he ran a hand through his oiled hair. He was youthful and quite handsome in appearance, at the sight of us, his face dissolved into a relieved boyish grin. He energetically shook our hands.

"Oh, thank goodness, monsieur's! When Philippe had promised to help me I had thought he would send the police - but the great Sherlock Holmes! This is wonderful, Christine will soon be discovered."

"When did you last see Christine, Viscount?" Holmes asked.

"Two days ago. I had left Christine in her dressing room after I had taken her out for dinner."

"What was her temperament like?"

"Happy. She was going to play the role of Juliet in Romeo and Juliet, a role La Carlotta normally played."

"And what did you do after you left her in the dressing room?"

"I returned home."

"Nothing else"

"... No monsieur. I must go; I wish to search the opera boxes once more."

Raoul de Chagny departed and naturally Holmes wanted to investigate the last place Christine had been seen. The opera house's corridors were awash with stagehands and chorus girls; it was like battling a wave.

"Quite an innocent man for someone who has trained in the Navy," Holmes casually told me over his shoulder. "I suppose that is due to the education he received from his sisters and aunt; he has an effeminate air about him. His brother dotes on him, almost like another sister."

The Comte was more worried about Raoul than Christine, I wondered if he would do almost anything to avoid a scandal, perhaps even get rid of someone he thought was unsuitable for his brother.

"Not quite innocent enough to tell the truth though," Holmes continued. "He lied about what he did that night. I could see a distinct bruise barely hidden by his coat collar and the Comte told me that Raoul arrived home but soon left again on the evening of Christine's disappearance."

"Most curious," I murmured.

In front of Christine Daae's dressing room was a gaggle of ballet girls. They were giggling and whispering to each other, with a constant murmur of the 'opera ghost' passing their lips. They ignored Holmes and I when we tried to get past.

"I do so hope the opera ghost does not take an interest in dawdling ballet girls as well as singers!" Holmes announced loudly. The girls, loving the attention, shrieked dramatically and darted off, laughing, all except for one. The ballet dancer was moving from foot to foot, constantly in motion; her black hair was tightly tied up in a French bun.

"Are you monsieur Holmes?" She asked me.

"No, my dear," I said. "My good friend here is the person whom you are looking for."

She curtsied. "I am Meg Giry, Christine was my friend."

"'Was'?" Holmes queried.

"We argued just before she went missing and - oh - I'm so sorry."

She let out a small sob and I gently patted her arm.

"There, there, we'll find her."

"Why did you argue?" Holmes ploughed on.

"Christine has changed since her singing lessons with the opera ghost -"

"She's being taught by a ghost?" I asked in surprise.

"Every evening she would lock herself away in her room. I never saw anyone enter before her but when I pressed my ear to the door I heard a man's voice! It had to be a ghost." Meg rubbed at her eyes.

"Christine sounded like a goose before her singing lessons, now she is an angel. La Carlotta is furious because Christine has taken over most of her roles."

"And Christine" Holmes pressed. "How did she change?"

"At first she was like a girl in love, always sighing and looking in her mirror, but when the Viscount started courting her she became almost as conceited as Carlotta. She no longer saw herself as part of the chorus, she shunned us. It was only when she was in trouble that she turned to me for help."

"Which was..?"

"Christine confided in me that her teacher was the ghost. I called her a fool that the ghost was dangerous, and I was right. She became afraid of him... but I have no idea why." Meg curtsied once more. "Forgive me, I have to go. Since Christine's disappearance my mother has warned me not to travel without friends, though it's the oddest thing, she doesn't believe it is the opera ghost but an ordinary man! If it is then it must be the Persian, he is always skulking about the opera house for no apparent reason." Little Meg Giry scuttled away and we watched her retreating back.

"Quite a mine of information," I told my friend, who was rubbing his chin absentmindedly.

"Yet she did not tell us exactly why she and Christine argued," he replied. "I would be interested in speaking with Giry's mother; she seems to be the only person here with a level head. I'm quite curious about this 'Persian' as well."

We entered Christine Daae's dressing room and saw the masses of wilting white roses which covered every inch of the room. The room was overpowered with the scent of it and I felt vaguely light headed. How had the young woman managed to sleep with all of this surrounding her? Holmes rubbed a fallen petal in-between his thumb and fore finger.

"The same species of rose; the same black ribbon wrapped around each of them. They are all from one person."

"The Viscount" I wondered.

"He could afford it."

"Possibly... or could it be another admirer, one who became jealous."

At the back of the room was a large, almost as tall as Holmes, ornate mirror with roses carved into the frame. It reflected the entirety of the room.

"What a spectacular mirror!" I said as I peered into it. "No wonder Miss Daae looked at it, it's rather hard to ignore."

"Yes, it is, almost as though she was being constantly watched by her own reflection."

I watched as Holmes' reflection knelt to search underneath the bed. When he came back out, he clutched a handful of letters tied together with string.

"Read these for me Watson."

Holmes and I switched places, while I stood by the bed and read out the letters' contents, Holmes began examining the mirror. The seal was broken but I could still see that it had once been a red death's head. I shivered, what could be inside such a letter, threats? I opened the first one. They were words of love.

"'My dear Christine, my love for you is revealed every time you sing. I have crafted your voice into a magnificent instrument, all out of love. Will you not honor me with a private show?'

"It's signed by someone called 'O.G.', Holmes."

"O... G... Opera Ghost; what does the next one say?"

"'Christine, I saw you with that fop tonight. He was full of praises wasn't he? Little does he know that it is through my tuition; our secret. It is wonderful that you have friends that can see our talent Christine, but keep him at bay. O.G.'"

There were several more letters which were similar to the ones I have written down, however the later letters took a much darker turn.

"'You missed a lesson, Christine. I was most displeased. I will be even angrier if you missed it because of that foolish boy. I ought to ensure that he will never want to return to the opera house again, do you want me to do that? Is that why you tease me? You never let him into the dressing room, where I can see, but I know he is outside. You forget, my dear, I know everything that happens here. I see all.'"

I paused. "Goodness, Holmes! This man sounds unbalanced with jealousy."

"Yes, but is he a man of flesh or an apparition? Do ghosts usually write letters?" He was focused on one corner of the mirror. "How odd; there's a hairline fracture here yet it does not consist with someone hitting the mirror or throwing something at it. It is almost like a window pane when someone has shut the window too violently."

I wanted to find out more about this 'opera ghost' and so I began to question the ballet girls and stagehands. There was one person in particular who knew a lot about the ghost. Joseph Buquet had apparently seen him while working late one night. The man described him as being 'incredibly thin and wearing a dress coat' and that his head was not made of flesh but a 'death's head, with stretched skin and dark pits for eyes'. A fireman had once witnessed the opera ghost as well, when he had been asked to inspect the building. They had to carry the man out after he had fainted. The fireman had seen a skeleton, wearing a dress coat, whose head was aflame. I was deeply worried for the missing young woman. If she had been taken by the opera ghost, be he flesh or spirit, how would she fare if she rejected his 'love'? All worries were momentarily forced out of my head when a sudden squawk rang out across the opera house.

"I cannot believe this! Me, a suspect."

Holmes was standing before the opera house's grand staircase. There was a brightly dressed woman next to him; in her arms was a small and very furry dog which made a faint yapping noise. She had been the sudden loud voice. I had no idea what Holmes was saying to her. As I approached, I could hear him more clearly.

"La Carlotta, you are not the only suspect."

"I should not be one at all. If I had done away with this air-headed girl then I would have left her body upon these steps, but instead she is gone, most likely seeking attention and the production has been postponed. I have had enough of this! The managers are fools, they cannot see proper

THE CASE OF THE CRACKED MIRROR

talent, and I am going before I am accused of something else." Carlotta left as she quietly muttered to herself in Spanish.

"Not postponed," Holmes told me. "The managers have announced that they shall have to go on with the opera and that they will have Carlotta play the role of Juliet."

There were several suspects; Carlotta, furious at how easily her starring roles had been taken from her, might have hidden Christine away so that she could regain her former glory; Raoul had been the last person to see her and had lied about where he had been on the night of her disappearance; Philippe was an overprotective brother who might have believed that Christine was taking advantage of Raoul, while Meg and Christine had argued. And, of course, there was the opera ghost...

Meg's mother, Madame Giry, was the opera house's concierge. Holmes and I tracked her down in the corridor that led to the opera boxes; however Madame Giry was not alone. She was with a Persian gentleman; I assumed he was the person whom Meg had referred to. They eyed us warily as we approached.

"What can I do for you, monsieur?" The woman asked us. The Persian said nothing but he keenly watched Holmes with bright jade colored eyes, atop his head was an astrakhan cap.

"You do not believe that Christine Daae's disappearance is the fault of the opera ghost," Holmes began.

"No, I do not."

"Female intuition; or is it something else?"

Madame Giry looked at the boxes and then back at us. "I would not normally do this, however something terrible might happen to the girl if all of your time is spent chasing the ghost. I have spoken with him."

"With the ghost: where?" I asked. This ghost was a talkative chap, wasn't he?"

"In one of the opera boxes, I bring him his... his money."

"He is blackmailing you?"

"No doctor. It is his fee. All of the managers who have owned the opera house have had to pay the ghost his wage."

"Being paid to haunt somewhere, how strange"

"If not, then he will play tricks on the staff and try to ruin productions."

"And what does he look like?" Holmes questioned her. "I suspect it is not a skull aflame."

"I have no idea." Madame Giry made a non-committal

gesture. "I enter the box, I hear his voice, but he is not in the box. When I leave and return later, the money has vanished."

"Which box does he use?"

"No," she shook her head defiantly. "He will know if I tell you. However, he has no idea of Christine's whereabouts. Every single time I enter the box he constantly asks me where Christine is. Goodbye, monsieur's."

Madame Giry could run off as quickly as her daughter, soon enough we were left with the Persian.

"I would not trust anything that ghost says," the Persian's voice was gruff and heavily accented. A look of frustration passed over his face and I was briefly reminded of the world weary detective Lestrade whenever Holmes infuriated him. "If one is involved in blackmail then they will soon fall into kidnapping."

"Quite an odd ghost... I had thought being dead meant no longer needing material things," Holmes remarked. The Persian flushed and merely replied, "Nor would a ghost require trapdoors and passageways to get around."

"You know this ghost."

"I knew him before he became a ghost. I tell you sir, he is deranged and I shall not speak any more about this lest his tricks turn to violence. But remember this - keep your hand to your eyes when he is nearby!" The Persian left us.

"A man rather than a ghost," my friend concluded, "as I had thought." He went to box five and answered my curious expression. "It was this box that Madame Giry looked to when she spoke of the opera ghost, as though she was afraid he could hear her from here."

Inside of the opera box, where the rich and affluent watched the opera from down below, I could see that this was the best place to see the stage. I wondered how many times Christine had been gazed upon by this 'ghost' and not known he was watching her, a ghoulish thought.

Holmes was far too preoccupied with examining the box's walls. He knocked on each one until he came across a hollow sounding noise. He smiled grimly.

"Perhaps our elusive friend is watching us this very moment! If he has eyes and ears all about the opera house then that must mean he has a network - a network of hidden passageways inside of this building." Holmes had his ear pressed to the wall, listening. "This man must have either obtained a copy of the construction plans or been involved in the construction itself, I prefer the latter for who else would need these passages except for a ghost made of flesh?"

I believe Holmes was expecting a reply, why else would he try to antagonize the ghost? However, before anyone had the chance to speak, there was a sudden uproar outside of the boxes. I opened the door and peered outside, calling over a ballet girl who was searching for someone to gossip with. "Whatever is the matter?"

"It's Carlotta; she's lost her voice again!"

Holmes would not come downstairs to see whether or not it was true. He waved me away, too focused on finding a hidden doorway to the passages.

"I had expected something like this to happen," he told me. "It is no longer important now; I know who the culprit is."

"Who"

"It does not matter, everything will be resolved soon. It is paramount that I find a way inside though!"

I could not believe him, what if it would help us discover where Christine had gone off to? All he cared about was tricks and mechanisms. It was I who made my way down, back to the grand staircase, to find Carlotta weeping silently. She was surrounded by her admirers, a few of the ballet girls, Raoul and the managers - who looked the most distressed out of them all.

"Oh, whatever shall we do?" One of the managers said as

he wrung his hands, "one missing and the other mute! This will be a disaster!"

I noticed little Meg Giry amongst the group of ballerinas.

"Miss Giry."

She turned at the sound of my voice. The poor thing's cheeks were quite bloodless and her eyes darted around nervously. "It has happened again," she whispered fearfully to me. "Carlotta lost her voice a few months ago and Christine took over yet Christine is no longer here. Who is supposed to take Christine's place? Is... Is the opera ghost displeased with Christine in some way and wants her to be replaced?"

"Who knows?" I said, though I knew she would find more comfort in her theories than not knowing what was happening. "Holmes and I will find Christine; no one is going to replace her." Meg Giry nodded. When she saw the managers leave she followed after them, perhaps to ask them what they planned to do. Carlotta opened her mouth, in an attempt to sing, but all that came out was a croak. She dissolved into tears once more and I couldn't help but feel sorry for her. Raoul hurried over to me.

"Where is monsieur Holmes?" He asked me. "What has he discovered?"

"Holmes is upstairs, examining the opera boxes," I told him.

"We found a series of letters addressed to Christine, each missive declaring love to her."

"Well, they are certainly not from me. I would say it to her face."

"They are from the opera ghost -"

"Not that cursed rumor! Christine is not having an affair with him." He sighed and continued. "It's ridiculous. The gossips have made out that Christine has sold her soul to the dead for her voice."

"I'm afraid to say that it might be true," I was quick to explain. "The letters suggested that the opera ghost was her tutor, Christine even admitted it to a ballet girl. Holmes also believes the ghost is a man masquerading as a spirit."

"Then we must search for this man!"

Raoul grasped my arm and began to lead me up the stairs, in search of Holmes.

"And alert the authorities to flush him out."

We entered box five but Holmes was not in there and he wasn't in any of the other boxes. Raoul petulantly threw himself into a seat.

"Where is he? We have to hurry!"

"Calm down Viscount." I sat down in the plush red chair next to him. "Holmes will soon be back." I thought that I should try to get to the bottom of things; after all, the viscount was sporting a bruise and had lied about where he had been. "Does it hurt?"

"What?"

Surprisingly Raoul's hand went to his stomach instead of his collar.

"I don't know what you're talking about."

"Your brother told Holmes that you were nowhere to be found on the night of Christine's disappearance." Raoul buried his face into his hands.

"It has nothing to do with this. It was simply..."

"Yes?"

"Shameful. I can't believe I acted so terribly."

"Tell me what happened." Raoul pulled down his coat collar to reveal a faint bruise that could only have come from a noose.

"Philippe did not tell you everything. When I came home my brother and I argued over Christine. I had voiced my desire to marry her and he disapproved. Philippe had told me that it was fine to have 'fun' with her but I could not marry a singer. We came to blows and so I left before either of us did something we would regret." He gently touched his neck. "I received this later in the evening. I had gone to the nearest club and drank as much as the owner would let me; soon I had wandered to the opera house, with a wine bottle clutched in my hand, and... Oh, what a fool I am! I had gone to the lower part of the building and started calling for the ghost to come out and face me."

"I assume he appeared."

"Yes, it was a man wearing a mask. All I remember was a rope going around my neck and desperately struggling against it. I collapsed and when I awoke I had been dumped amongst some old stage scenery. Someone had given me a beating." Raoul lifted up his shirt, enough for me to see the deep bruises across his stomach and chest. "Please, do not be angry with me for having kept this from you. It had nothing to do with Christine's disappearance and I was embarrassed at how foolish I had been."

"It is a lucky thing that you survived," Holmes' voice boomed from all around us. "This phantom sees you as a love rival and I do not believe this man is above murder."

"Holmes!" I started from my chair. "Where are you?"

"I am right here with you, doctor." Holmes laughed. Then the wall to the right, the wall Holmes had been examining, swung open. Holmes climbed out. In the span of twenty minutes he had managed to tear his trousers and coat, lost his hat, and covered himself from head to toe in dust and cobwebs.

"You look a mess."

"Thank you, Watson." He sat down in the chair I had been

sitting in moments before his arrival. "Now Viscount, Christine is safe and will be returned to you this evening."

"Safe? How can you be certain? Where is she?"

"The person who has Christine does not wish to harm her."

"Who is it?" Raoul said with gritted teeth.

"That is up to Christine Daae to say. However, I will tell you this; there are many more passageways where you encountered the ghost." Holmes did not have to say anything else. Raoul, in the belief that his love could be in one of these passages, arose and went off in search of them. "That will give us enough time to find Miss Daae," Holmes told me. "Walk with me, Watson, I shall tell you what I saw." We had left the opera house. I had no idea where we were going but Holmes was intent on something. "Erik can see and hear everything in the opera house because of his passageways," he said as we walked.

"Erik?"

"The opera ghost, If Erik was not the kidnapper then it meant that she was taken outside of the building, where he could not see. The kidnapper lured Christine out of her dressing room. It had to be someone Christine knows."

In the distance I saw a cloaked figure. Was that the one we were following?

"I found the door to the box's passageway, which was quite ingenious; no one besides myself would think to look behind there. It was a shame you had left me to my own devices, I can imagine the gothic prose you would have used to describe it to your readers. The words which come to mind are 'desolate', 'unnerving' and 'haunting'," Holmes recounted.

"Holmes." I frowned at him; my writings in the Strand were a constant amusement to him.

"I ended up in Christine's dressing room, from behind the mirror! You were right when you said it was hard to ignore it, the ghost has most likely been watching the singer from behind the glass for quite a while."

"How shocking, it sounds like something from a lurid novel."

"I quickly deduced that the hairline fracture I had found came from slamming the mirror too hard. My wanderings through Erik's network soon alerted him to my presence though. He came upon me suddenly, as silent as a ghost, and my life would have been forfeit had I not remembered the Persian's words. I raised my hand to my eyes. A rope wrapped around my wrist and neck, intent on strangling me. With my hand in-between the rope and my throat, I was able to pull it off. It was then that I saw my attacker. The figure led us to a graveyard. We quickened our pace. It was a masked man. We grappled and it was only when I had him rammed against the wall that I could knock off his mask."

"What was underneath?"

"A deformity, one so severe, that it gives him the appearance of a corpse. The loss of his mask seemed to take away his resolve. He crumpled to the floor, sobbing and clutching his face. We spoke, briefly, but I did not stay for long. The shock of losing his mask was steadily draining away."

It was a crypt that the figure opened and entered. Inside, someone had lit a candle and what we saw was Christine Daee safe and well. She was wrapped up in a coarse and dirty blanket and she was whispering with the kidnapper. Her eyes, wide and doe-like, looked up and she gasped. The kidnapper turned, revealing it was the ballerina Meg Giry. I could not believe it. At the sight of us she gave a cry of fear and made to run but Christine stopped her.

"Meg - Meg! You knew this could not have worked."

Meg Giry collapsed into Christine's arms. "I'm sorry, I'm so sorry, Christine."

"This was about jealousy," Holmes murmured to me. "However, it was not a matter of the heart but ambition. I suppose Carlotta's sudden muteness is down to the Giry girl as well."

"It is," Meg admitted. "The ghost had paid mama to drug Carlotta a few months ago, so that Christine could take her part. I used what was left in the bottle."

"But why would you do this?" I asked. "Your own friend"

"I just..." Meg sniffed. "I wanted to be as loved as Christine was. My voice is as good as hers yet no one has ever given me the chance to sing. I thought if I could keep Christine away until the day of the performance then I could step in. I'm going to be arrested, aren't I?"

"Oh, Meg" Christine said and the two girls embraced.

"There's no need to tell anyone what you did."

"What shall we do now?" I wondered. "Surely they will want an explanation as to where Christine has been."

"I went away for a while," Christine suggested, as she ran a hand through Meg's hair. "I had no idea that I would cause so much distress."

"Really Christine" Meg whispered. "You would do that for me?"

"I once considered pushing Carlotta down the stairs because I wanted to play Juliet," the singer told her.

"I understand what you're feeling. It's going to take some

time before I forgive you but you can't earn that forgiveness in a cell." She kissed her on her brow. "Let's go back to the opera house. I want to see Raoul."

The matter of Christine's disappearance was soon swept under the carpet. Meg was constantly at Christine's side, desperate to be forgiven for her folly. Raoul soon proposed to Christine and the pair was to be married. However, Holmes would become pensive whenever I mentioned the Paris Opera house.

"There is still the opera ghost," he once said in reply. "He might not have been involved in this incident but he is far from docile."

It was only when, during that time known as the Great Hiatus, that I opened the newspaper and read about the terrible tragedy that befell the opera house. A masked madman, intent on stealing away a singer, had dropped a chandelier upon the audience...

SHERLOCK HOLMES

A Strange Affair with the Woman on the tracks

Holmes was not amused. Mycroft had visited 221B Baker Street last week and I had watched with mild impatience as the pair bickered. "Will you get to the point, brother?" Holmes had finally said once he had seen Mycroft start to 'adjust' one of his experiments. "I assume you have somewhere else you would prefer to be." "Indeed I do," Mycroft replied. "I need you to follow a man we suspect has taken some rather important documents. We believe that they are going to be sold to an enemy country." We were supposed to attend an event that was going to take place on a steam locomotive.

Mycroft handed us the invitation and tickets he had managed to acquire, not giving Holmes the chance to argue his way out of this. "It's not your usual train journey," he had warned Holmes. "You will have to keep an eye on Kells no matter what."

Now, a week later, we were seated in the train's dining car, a table away from the suspect. Smoke wafted past the windows as the train picked up speed. An unquiet machine, the train let out a variety of whistles and moans, with the constant murmur of the wheels chugging along. However, a short while after we had left the station the train began to slow and then crawl to a stop. The reason for Holmes' annoyance was due to what he had just heard. We had followed our suspect into a parlor game. The train had stopped midway on its journey and our 'host' had arisen, announcing that the murder mystery was about to begin. Mycroft had an ironic sense of humor.

The host was a young man, I recognized him as being the son of Conservative MP Charles Hourbun, and standing next to him was his wife. She was quite pale and her eyes were wide and luminous. The woman smiled faintly at me when she noticed me looking at her. Her husband, I believe his name was James Hourbun, ran a hand through his dark slicked back hair.

"On this very railway line, on this very train, there was an awful tragedy," he began. "A woman fell on the tracks and was instantly killed." A faint murmur washed over the guests. Their interest was piqued. "It has always been assumed that this was an unfortunate accident, however, was it actually murder? I hope you enjoy yourselves as we will be reenacting that fateful night. We even have an actual detective attending, may I introduce Mr. Sherlock Holmes and his good friend doctor Watson!" The guests clapped and Holmes grudgingly bowed his head in acknowledgement.

The train had stopped between Sheringham and Holt. This was where the supposed murder had taken place. The basis was that fifty years ago, in eighteen forty four, the train had encountered a tree on the tracks, for several hours they were stuck until the workers had managed to remove it. The train ploughed on...

One of the train's passengers had left the train when it had stopped and wandered onto the track, she was crushed by the wheels before the train could halt. I had heard of this tale before, though I had thought it had been based on another track. When the railway company had begun laying tracks in the countryside villagers were outraged. In some areas houses and small businesses would have to be pulled down to make way for the railway line. To retaliate, people protested against the sprawl of train tracks which they felt were ruining the serenity of the English countryside, and had begun to spread ghoulish rumors about accidents and murders on the tracks in an attempt to ruin business. However, it appears to have had the opposite effect...

"I wouldn't be surprised if they announced a séance next," Holmes whispered to me. "A funny place for a handover, isn't it? Perhaps that is the appeal - who would suspect it to happen under the guise of a parlor game?" The suspect, Kells, who had a prominent bald patch and a greying moustache, constantly looked over his shoulder at us. He returned to his glass of whiskey. "However shall we catch them at it?" I whispered back to Holmes. "Surely they will be on guard after Hourbun's introduction?" "Either the pair will become so desperate that they will throw caution to the wind or I shall acquire the documents some other way. Mycroft's only concern is the return of these papers."

I glanced around the dining car. Seated at each of the tables amongst the scones, coffee and sandwiches were all people I recognized from the newspapers. There were a few minor politicians, a German and Italian diplomat, the wife and eight year old son of a silk merchant as well as an up and coming journalist. I wondered who Kells planned to trade the papers with. The politicians were all seated together; their voices were a quiet drone as they discussed politics. Holmes had already deduced that one had a very severe opium addiction while another was a secret Liberal. The journalist, who was sitting at the table opposite to us and writing down everything he could hear, was desperately looking for a story to top the political scandal he had exposed the year before. Though, according to Holmes, he was not doing so well with his career from the look of his faded and patched up suit. Holmes had also noticed that the silk merchant's wife had taken off her ring. Who knew what would be revealed about their marriage in the gossip columns within the next few weeks? Even though the German and Italian diplomats sat at the same table, their body language showed that they would much rather sit elsewhere. It was quite an odd array of people.

Hourbun sat down next to me and greeted us cheerfully. It was hard to imagine him as being Charles Hourbun's son; the man was a rather grim gentleman who had no time for the lower classes. In comparison James Hourbun was like sunshine or a well natured barman.

"I hadn't expected to see you here, Mr. Holmes."

"Neither did I, this event came recommended to me by my brother... he told me it was quite interesting."

"Jolly good. This is the second 'mystery' I have hosted. I was actually inspired by your writings, doctor."

"Why, thank you," I said. "I hope to make this a regular event. It would do marvelously in the holidays."

"What made you decide to use trains?" Holmes asked.

"My grandfather actually contributed to this steam locomotive and the track. He loved trains. I often ride the Sheringham to Holt, just so I am reminded of him. It was my grandfather who told me the 'woman on the tracks' rumor and it used to terrify me as a child."

"Do you happen to know that man over there?" Holmes indicated to Kells.

"I believe we've met but I'm not quite certain."

James Hourbun craned his neck to look at the man behind us. "That's William Kells," Hourbun answered. "My godfather, He works for one of the government departments, something important though I'm not sure what. He has always been a little nervy. Anyway, I must get everything organized." He stood and approached another table, the one where the German and Italian diplomats sat.

The train journey had started early in the evening and as it was summer, it was still quite light. However, since then it had steadily darkened. Outside, when I looked out of the train window, all I could see were the tracks leading off into the night, almost as though it had disappeared into the void. It was the time when creatures from the unknown would begin to awaken.

A table was brought into the middle of the room. Holmes had been right; they were going to conduct a séance!

Holmes watched, bemused, as an Ouija board was placed down. It was a finely crafted item, with the words, letters and numbers being carved into the board amongst rose and skull designs.

"Gather round, everyone," Hourbun told us. The mother of the young boy shook her head; she pulled her son back when he tried to examine the Ouija board.

"I'd rather not get involved, sir," she said. "It goes against my beliefs."

"Very well, Mrs. Cavell, but it is merely harmless fun."

Hourbun's wife wasn't interested in the Ouija board either. She sat down at one of the other tables, intending on being a spectator.

Chairs were placed around the table and it was quite a tight squeeze for us all even without Mrs. Cavell, her son and Hourbun's wife. I was placed between Holmes and Hourbun, while Kells had been seated next to Holmes. The man swallowed and tugged at his collar, for a moment I could have sworn he meant to check his pockets. Hourbun grinned in excitement as he told us to hold hands. Holmes couldn't help but smirk at me as he held mine and Kells' hands. In my left hand, Hourbun's palm felt cold and clammy. I noticed a faint tremor. I curiously watched him, was the young man ill? Or was he nervous due to ensuring that everything went along smoothly?

"Spirits from the other side come towards our voices. Listen to us, answer our questions." He dropped his hands and we took that as our cue to do the same. We each placed a finger a top the planchette on the Ouija board. "Is the spirit of the unfortunate woman who died here on the tracks with us?" Hourbun said to thin air. The planchette, a small piece of wood which resembled a heart, shivered and began to move. I glanced at Holmes out of the corner of my eye but he was too focused on Kells, subtly, of course. 'Yes', the planchette moved over. "Did a murder take place on the night of your death?" There was a pause, then... 'Yes'. "Who murdered you?" It began to spell out words. 'Their', 'name', 'is' -

The door leading to the passenger car banged open and a woman strode out. She ignored us, she was too furious to notice anything around her. Her hair streamed behind her as she moved around us. The black dress she wore swirled about as she looked around agitatedly. "I cannot believe this!" She said over her shoulder to the gentleman who had just followed after her. "You and that woman; you have shamed me Henry. How can I marry you now?" "Jane, wait!" The man made to grasp Jane's wrist but she shook him off. "It meant nothing!"

Jane and Henry disappeared into the next compartment.

We were silent, perhaps in slight shock. Then Holmes chuckled and I soon realized what had happened. A re-enactment, 'Jane' and 'Henry' must have been hired actors from the stage to make this tale feel even more real. James Hourbun certainly had an imaginative mind. Mrs. Cavell was fanning herself; her son buried his face into her skirt, the politician who Holmes suspected had an opium addiction looked extremely unsettled, while Hourbun's wife appeared to be silently laughing. Holmes leaned over to peer after Jane and Henry pressing slightly against Kells. I saw his hand briefly dip into the man's pocket but come away empty. The Ouija board was put away and everyone started to relax.

"Henry and his fiancée, Jane, had taken the train to Holt when it suddenly stopped due to a tree on the tracks. They would be married in the church Jane had been christened in. It was then, in a fit of guilt, Henry admitted to having an affair. Jane fled the train in a rage and Henry chased after her," Hourbun narrated. "What did they do next?" The light flickered and suddenly went out; it was all too coincidental to be an accident. Someone began to panic and I couldn't see where Holmes had got to. "Look, over there!" Mrs. Cavell cried out. She clutched her son close to herself. Several faces peered out of the windows, myself included.

There was a woman, wearing a light colored dress, wandering across the tracks! She stumbled but did not fall. In the darkness she was the most noticeable thing out there, however I saw a dark figure a few steps behind her. The glow of the moonlight fell over the woman as she walked further away from us. It had to be the actress from before yet she wore a completely different costume. A match flared and revealed Hourbun as he opened the door which led outside. "Follow her then!" He called out enthusiastically. "How else will we discover the truth?" We disembarked and made our way across the tracks. Hourbun did not join us. I was sure that Holmes had remained on the train also, however I could barely see in front of me so I could not be entirely certain. Our only source of light was the match and we were steadily moving away from it. Someone bumped into me. I held them steady and squinted my eyes. It was William Kells. I let go of him but made certain to stay nearby. Mycroft had warned us not to let him out of our sight. If Holmes was not here then it was down to me to keep an eye on him. Briefly I looked over my shoulder back at the halted train. It too was plunged into darkness; all I could see was its faint outline. For a moment, a very unnerving moment, I half expected the lights to come back on and the train to suddenly start - crushing us all just as the woman in the rumor was. A ridiculous thought.

We stumbled over the line, following the actors Hourbun had hired for this game. Amongst the sound of labored breathing and our footsteps, the man, Henry, was calling out for Jane to stop - that he loved her - that it had meant nothing. Jane did not speak. There was a faint touch on my arm, a whisper. In the gloom I could just barely see Hourbun's wife. She appeared frightened... perhaps she too was a little nervous at walking on the tracks. "It's alright," I told her. "The train won't start up again." She looked back at the train but said nothing. Her hair blew in a breeze though I had felt no wind. We walked for several minutes, until the train's outline finally faded. It was then that we reached the actors. Someone had lit a lamp and placed it by their feet. Henry and Jane stood facing one another, arguing. There were tears running down the woman's face. "How could you Henry?" She sobbed, her hands kept on clenching and unclenching. She was trapped between sorrow and anger. "I gave everything to you." "I know, Jane." He cupped her face. "That woman was nothing, Sarah was nothing -" "Sarah My sister?!"

Jane screeched at this further betrayal and went for Henry. They began to struggle. Henry was the stronger out of the two yet the woman's pain was unstoppable. His hands wrapped around her throat and Jane clawed at his face until she fell. She lay there, across the tracks, and was quite still. Mrs. Cavell gasped in shock and Henry ran past us back to the train. We stared down at Jane's body.

It had seemed all too real, had they really been acting? I knelt down next to her and felt for a pulse. She opened one eye and grinned at me, pointing to the train. "It's alright, sir," she quietly told me. "No need to call the police today!" The lights had returned, thankfully the train was stationary. When we entered the train I saw Henry sitting at one of the tables, languidly smoking a cigarette and sipping whisky. Next to him was Holmes, his curved pipe in hand, and the pair were happily chatting. I frowned at Holmes as Kells came inside, had my friend spent the entire time in the dining car? I knew he often enjoyed spiting his brother; however would he risk our country's welfare over a petty spat?

I was the first to enter the train and so I could ascertain that the two diplomats, a politician, Holmes and Hourbun had remained on the train. My gaze drifted across those who had walked on the tracks; the remaining politicians, Mrs. Cavell, her son, the journalist, Hourbun's wife, and Kells and I. Although I had tried to stay close to Kells I knew that he could have easily slipped the documents to another person, it had been too dark to see.

After a few minutes Jane appeared. Hourbun clapped. "A round of applause for Henry Marns and Jane Frau, for they did their best no matter how strange my requests." Henry went to stand next to Jane, the pair held hands and bowed and we applauded them. The parlor game had ended and it was time to ride to Holt, with a whistle the train began its steadfast journey. Outside trees and countryside, shadowed and dangerous looking in the night, flew past us as it picked up speed. I sat down opposite Holmes and I had no idea what my friend planned to do. Everyone else had found their seats from before. Mrs. Cavell was biting her lip while her son was happily cheering for more to occur. Quite a ghoulish child, what he wanted to see was another death. I shook my head and wondered if I too had been like that. Henry and Jane had disappeared back in the passenger car; apparently they were no longer needed. Hourbun was incredibly pleased with himself and Kells' nerves seemed to have calmed slightly. Had we missed our chance? Were the papers now in someone else's possession? "What about the papers?" I whispered to Holmes. "Are they even here?"

"They are here," Holmes told me with a cryptic smile. "Wait and see."

It was hard to be patient; Holmes would not answer a single question. When the train finally reached Holt station, I watched as the passengers disembarked. I struck them off of my suspect list as each individual left unhindered by Holmes. It was obvious, I felt, that Mrs. Cavell and her son were not involved. She loudly announced that she would never partake in another of these events, that it had given her and her son a years' worth of nightmares. Then the politicians stepped off, they moved away from the train in a tight group, it reminded me of ants or schoolboys staying close while on a school trip.

I had noticed, on the way to Holt that something strange was happening between the diplomats. They had sat with one another again; however they were increasingly becoming annoyed. Not with one another but in regards to a different matter. Earlier on they had constantly glared at the other, now they quietly colluded. The journalist was about to leave while looking a little crestfallen, when Holmes called out to him."Mr Fen, I suggest you stay here. I should like a witness for this." Fen looked at him curiously as he resumed sitting. Hourbun's curiosity was also piqued, as was mine. The man's smile had stiffened.

"What is the matter Mr. Holmes? Is anything wrong?"

"You're very fond of forging things, aren't you Mr. Hourbun?"

Hourbun looked even more confused and it was then that the German diplomat arose in a furious rage.

"I knew it!" He roughly barked out at Hourbun. "You, sir, are a fraud. Give me back my money!"

What on earth was happening? The diplomat grasped Hourbun's jacket and seemed ready to strike him, his newfound friend, the Italian diplomat, was also intent on ensuring that Hourbun did not escape them. The rage, sparked by what Holmes had hinted at, had made them reckless, they didn't care who heard them. Mr. Fen was agog while Kells kept on eyeing the exit. Hourbun raised his hands in a peaceful gesture. "Chaps, I have no idea what he is speaking of," he nervously said. "The papers are fakes Hourbun," the German diplomat snarled. "And the men of my family do not allow mere boys to make them into fools!" "Ah, then they prefer to be criminals?" That was Mycroft's voice!

Holmes' brother stepped onto the train; he was flanked by detective Lestrade and a police officer. As usual Mycroft looked faintly irritated, most likely at having to appear in public, while Lestrade seemed curious to see what exactly Holmes had done this time. "The papers Sherlock" Mycroft asked as he wiped his face with his handkerchief. "You mean these?" From Holmes' coat pocket he produced a sheath of documents, the stolen papers.

William Kells, the two diplomats and even James Hourbun were taken in by the police for questioning. As Holmes and I waited for the train to London to arrive he explained to me what exactly had transpired. "Hourbun's little game had nothing to do with keeping alive a fond memory of his grandfather. What he had planned was a regular meeting point for his contacts while using the event as a cover. Kells, Hourbun's godfather, would steal classified documents and Hourbun would act as the middle man. Men, like the two diplomats, would bid for the documents. The bidding started the moment your group was led outside of the train." "They did this in front of you?" I asked in disbelief. Holmes chuckled and shook his head. "No, they made certain that I was not privy to their hushed conversation, however why else would the two diplomats be so hostile to one another and intent upon something then, afterwards, one was left scowling and sulking while the other exuded triumph?"

"But I saw you check Kells' pocket," I said, still incredibly bewildered. "And how did you end up with the actual documents while they had a forgery?"

"I had intended on a switch from the start. This morning, with Mycroft's input, I created a not so perfect replica to enrage the winning bidder. I was hopeful for the German diplomat, he has become known for his short fuse. However, I now had to find the documents to perform the switch. Do you remember when those two actors brushed past us at the séance?"

"Yes."

"When we were seated for the séance I checked Kells pocket, the papers were in there, yet I couldn't make the switch immediately. Then, when I tried again, after the lights had gone out, the papers had vanished."

"What had happened to them?"

"I suppose, in a bid to conceal them from me, the handover had to be done where there were enough witnesses - witnesses who would swear they hadn't seen any papers being exchanged. Jane Frau had to push past Kells to get past, Hourbun had told her to lift the papers from him and leave them in her dress."

"That would explain the costume change."

"It was Henry who told me why she had to change costumes. I, of course, realized what had happened. When everyone was distracted by Jane leaving the train I swapped the real papers with the fakes and swiftly returned to my seat. Then I simply had to wait."

"So that's how you figured it out," I paused and mulled it over. "Then, how was the journalist involved?"

"He wasn't. I thought I'd give him a lifeline, though I'm afraid Mycroft will be most displeased. He had been desperate that this all remained confidential."

"Holmes," I chided him, knowing full well the only reason why he had helped Fen was to annoy his brother.

"Yes, Watson" He answered innocently. "Ah, look, our trains arrived."

A gust of steam and smoke blew into our faces as the train drew up. Such a magnificent machine, no matter what bloodied tales those against it conjured up. Men and women in the distance rushed towards us, desperate to ensure they did not miss their train. "I almost cannot believe Hourbun was involved," I told Holmes as we embarked. "I wonder if his wife was also a part of it".

"Wife"

"The woman with Hourbun, she was pale and a little sickly in appearance."

"Hourbun has never been married," Holmes said to me, he watched me with interest. "He has no ring on his finger. Besides, the only women on the train were Mrs. Cavell and Jane Frau."

I blinked in shock, uncertain of what I had witnessed this evening. I had seen a woman no one else had seen, I had even spoken with her. My thoughts returned to her expression as she had looked back at the train, had it been fear? Terror that the train would come hurtling down and crush her once more, had the rumor of the woman on the tracks been true..?

I can only leave that to you dear reader, to decide upon with the account I have given to you. I will tell you this though, although I never saw her again on the Sheringham to Holt line, there have been many others who have written about her. Perhaps, if you are about to embark on a train journey, you should keep your eyes open for her.

SHERLOCK HOLMES

The Curse of a Native

I did not realize just how much I had missed Dr. John Watson until he came to the door and beamed at me before taking my hat and coat.

"You were supposed to be back a week ago," was his greeting.

I carefully lit my pipe even before sitting down.

"Didn't lose any opportunities to poison yourself I see, "He continued with his usual cynicism frequently displayed over the years about my smoking habit.

I finally sat down delighted to be back home and looked at

him trying my upmost not to allow any expression on my face that would give away anything or give away any clues.

"Don't tell me. Somehow on holiday out there in the African bush, some case came up".

I nodded back looking rather pleased with myself, "Very perceptive my dear Watson, very perceptive."

"These cases do follow you around the world then don't they? Who would have guessed that some minor case of burglary would come up at some remote gaming lodge in Africa?"

"Not burglary my dear Watson but suspected murder, I am hoping that you can work it out for me, as I did."

I had punished the man enough and so I settled down to give him the details of the strange murder in the most beautiful place I had ever been too in the heart of the African bush just days before my holiday was due to come to an end.

I have to admit that I had become quite fond of John Adams, the chain smoking American who loved his beer and recounting tales of his encounters with the high and mighty including royalty. His hearty laugh at the end of almost all his tales was rather infectious. And so when I came down for breakfast at the gaming lodge one morning and found him sprawled on the floor of the dining area dead and surrounded by shocked guests, I was more than a little distressed. His face was still twisted in pain and he was clearly foaming from his mouth, his other hand still clutching desperately at his stomach.

"Poisoned; Poor fellow." Watson interrupted me.

"Elementary my dear Watson, obviously so," I responded.

Adams was on holiday with his wife, son, and daughter-in-law. Naturally I started by interviewing them. His wife Rose was surprisingly young to be the wife of Adams in actual fact, younger than his son's wife. She said she had come down for breakfast and found Adams son, Peter and his wife Lorna already half way through their breakfast. She recalled that her husband asked why they were so early and Peter said that they were going on some game drive. Apparently Adams was in high spirits and sat down to sip his tea. A few minutes later he excused himself to go to the wash room. Rose did not think anything was amiss until he came out of the wash room and staggered as he walked back to the table. She found that strange since he had not taken any strong drink since waking up. He sat at the table obviously trying very hard to conceal his agony. But soon it must have gotten unbearable because he started clutching his stomach and moaning in pain. As luck would have it there was no doctor in the hotel, he had left the day before on some long game drive and had yet to return. Somebody suggested he be given some warm milk but before it could arrive from the kitchen he was on the floor. She watched helplessly as Adams died right there on the floor. It all happened so fast.

"I have not lived for years with Sherlock Holmes for nothing. In cases like this you need NOT look further than your spouse for the villain," Watson piped out.

"Precisely, my dear Watson, but as I have always told you; I never guess. It is a shocking habit. — Destructive to the logical faculty. Beware of the obvious which may not always be as obvious as you think."

Further interrogation revealed that Rose, twenty five years of age had married Adams, fifty, for his money. One would imagine that she was now going to come into immense financial wealth as his surviving widow.

I was already trying to work out how she had gotten the poison in to his tea undetected and yet they had come down to breakfast together. At the time, I had told myself it was possible that this was the area I would have to focus my intellect for this simple open-and-shut-wife-murders-husband for his money case. But I did not have all the facts. And neither did I want to get myself in to the situation of twisting the facts to fit the theory. Admittedly there was plenty I did not know at the time which would prove that such conclusions were presumptuous and possibly erroneously so...

Peter Adams was inconsolable and was still in tears as I interviewed him. He clearly loved his late father to bits. He told me that he had never understood what had come over him to marry Rose thirty years his junior and obviously a gold digger to everybody else but his father who adored her. He had come down to breakfast early when the tables were still being laid and did not notice anything unusual until his father started writhing in agony. No, he did not see Rose put anything in his tea but he was sure that she had to be responsible in some way for his father's death. Lorna corroborated her husband's version of events but she added that she did not think Rose was capable of murder; further interrogation of the murder unearthed the fact that she was a close friend of Rose, close enough for her to have clouded judgment over what she was capable or not capable of doing. But I had not even finished interviewing Lorna when the manager, a burly red head Mr. Butler who had the hairiest hands you can imagine, burst in and proclaimed that they had already caught the murderer. He led me out of the main building in to the servants' quarters to show me a native waiter called Kimilu. They had already tied his hands and legs together with some rope and had sent word to the police constable whom lived about fifty miles away from the gaming reserve. Apparently, the day before Adams had complained about the waiters' incompetence with always getting his orders mixed up; Mr. Butler admitted that Kimilu was the best waiter on his small staff and that is why he assumed that being from the American South, Adams' had a deep hatred for anybody dark skinned and that is what it was all about. He had seen this kind of thing on numerous occasions before and he always did the same thing. He told his valued visitors that the waiter had been sacked and they were simply kept out of site until the said guest departed. Only that this particular case was different. Adams had violently slapped Kimilu so hard that the sheer force had floored the waiter and the usually humble waiter had lost it. He had stood up and angrily talked back at him in his native language which Adams did not understand. But Butler had lived in Africa for over two decades and he understood every word. His translation confirmed by other native workers who witnessed the drama. It was chilling to say the least.

"In our tribe a man is never ever slapped. Never ever; you have hated and accused me for no reason. The sun shall not set tomorrow before you join your ancestors. Your death will be agonizing and you will writhe in pain on the very ground I unjustly landed on when you hit me. No body shall be able to save you. Others shall watch in horror but it will not matter even if the white man gives you his best medicine and magic potion, you will die. This is what was proclaimed as justice for what you have done by my ancestors and my ancestors have never been proved wrong. If this does not come to pass, I myself will die before sunset tomorrow. My ancestors have spoken."

Butler looked at me triumphantly before adding, "Kimilu comes from the Masai Tribe. They are experts with plants and herbs. He must have gotten some herbs from the bush and somehow slipped it in to Mr. Adams tea. You will have noted that whatever killed Adams was potent because he died very quickly."

It made sense, neatly so. Except for one minor detail; what Kimilu had said had sounded like some curse rather than a threat. My dear Watson the two are not the same thing. But then, this was Africa and I am not familiar with Africa.

I asked Kimilu about the incident through a translator. He pointed out that Adams was already in a bad mood because he had been shouting even before he served him lunch with his son. The two were dining alone. He had no idea what the quarrel was about and he said that he heard Adams use the word 'intestine' several times. Peter denied that he had argued with his father and added that they had certainly not discussed any 'intestines.'

I asked Mr. Butler where he was during breakfast and if he had noticed anything unusual. He said he was right there the whole time supervising breakfast and was busy mostly in the kitchen which is where he was when he heard a commotion amongst his guests and rushed back to find Adams gasping his last breath on the floor. Next, I asked him if he could figure out how the poison had gotten in to Adams' tea with his son and daughter-in-law seated at the table the whole time. To which he answered that he too was puzzled and would only speculate that it had been slipped in to his cup in the kitchen and was so potent that all it needed was for somebody to pour out the tea in the cup. He admitted that he had personally placed Mr. Adams tea cup at his usual place on the table fearing that he would start another row if he discovered that it was a native who had prepared and set his tea cup.

"Any thoughts at this juncture Watson"

"I would take a closer look at this Mr. Butler and explore possible motives he may have to murder one of his own guests. There is plenty of mischief that happens out there in the African bush."

"It didn't make any sense to me my dear Watson. But I still checked. The gaming lodge is in excellent financial footing; Hardly surprising since it is so bloody expensive. I would not afford it on my own and as you know the holiday was a gift from one of my rather grateful clients. Now why on earth would Mr. Butler spoil all that by murdering a wealthy client and giving himself the kind of publicity that will almost certainly keep away his treasured guests and threaten the financial stability he currently enjoys."

"Then he must surely hold the key to the mystery. The key has to be the cup and the happenings in and around it shortly before Adams came down for breakfast."

"I agree Watson. The key is the cup but you will need to look elsewhere for the answers. But even as I was putting my thoughts together something else happened. Peter Adams came to me accusing his step mother of the murder. He pointed out that he had discovered that she had gone to great lengths to contact the solicitors. They had gone in to the nearest town the following day with the car that took away Kimilu in to police custody where Butler had assured us that the police would get the whole truth from the native using methods he would rather not talk about. Rose had gone in to the post office and placed a long distance call to the solicitors to enquire about Mr. Adams' will before the body of her husband was hardly cold. When I got to her, she admitted that she had placed the call and had been told that it was not possible for her to get the information she wanted over the phone. That was not how wills were administered. Rose was frightened over what she had done but she uttered something that made plenty of sense although it did not exonerate her from the murder."

"Why would I kill my husband without knowing or being sure of the contents of his will? That wouldn't be very clever would it?

"But what was even more interesting was a confession by Peter Adams that would have meant nothing to a lesser mind. Alcohol is a clever detective's best friend because it loosens the tongue considerably. All one has to do is get as relaxed as possible with the subject and talk about anything and everything; which is precisely what I did.

Peter talked rather bitterly about his childhood and ended up blurting out that he was not Adams' biological son and had in fact been adopted when his mother got married to the American millionaire. He was only four years old then.

That statement my dear Watson burst the case right open.

Peter was obviously very fond of Adams. I could tell that with certainty. And yet he talked about mistreatment from Adams during his early childhood. He talked about a macabre incident where he was sent out in to the dark of the night to search for a key he had lost while playing in his tree house. He described the incident with rather vivid evidence that it had stuck in his mind for years and had never left him. His mother had been distressed and he could hear her sob as an angry Mr. Adams shoved him out in to the night and locked the door knowing fully well that he was always terrified of the dark. He was trembling in fright as he tip toed to the tree house but somehow his mother's helpless sobs had given him strength. With his heart still beating violently against his chest, he had desperately searched the tree house and found the key. And over the years he had also found love for his brute of a father, or had he?

So who murdered my friend John Adams? Kimilu, the native waiter out of blind rage? Rose, his gold digger of a wife? Peter, his loving step son, or Lorna his daughter-in-law? Or perhaps Mr. Butler the owner/manager?

My lab would have been considerable help in this case but being away in the middle of the bush in Africa I had no such luxury. It would have certainly helped me to interview Kimilu the waiter further but the language barrier and the lack of understanding of the local culture were a major obstacle to my using my usual methods."

"It would be understandable if this were the only case you never go to solve," Watson said," but as you say you solved the mystery. How did you do it may I ask?"

"A small detail Watson; it is always a small detail and it has to do with the alleged 'intestines.'

"Intestines" Watson was puzzled. "What intestines?"

"Remember that this was a native who had presumably never been to school and had only learnt English as a second language. In fact, just enough English to enable him to fulfill his duties as a waiter."

"Meaning"

"Meaning that you needed to look for a word similar to intestine."

"Well there are dozens of words similar in some way to the horrid word intestine."

"Actually not many that is connected to this case. Actually, I can only think of one."

"Now what word may that be?"

"Patience my dear Watson; You have several more minutes to find the word as I finish my African tale. I worked it all out but needed to prove my theory. And so I interviewed Rose, Lorna and Peter separately one last time. That order was important because I believe I would not have got the same results have I started with Peter. This is how the interview went".

Rose;

"Rose, did Mr. Adams leave a will?"

"I am not sure."

"Why do you say that?'

"He always said he would never write a will and get murdered for it."

"He said that?"

"Yes."

"Why then did you call his solicitor to ask if there was a will?"

"Because everybody said he has secretly written a will but did not want anybody to know about it."

Lorna;

"Lorna, did your father-in-law ever write a will?"

"No I don't think he did. But I can't be sure."

"What is it that you forgot in the room on the morning that your father-in-law died?"

"Who told you about that?"

"Just answer the question, please."

"It wasn't me, it was Peter's wallet."

"So he went back to the room for it?"

"No, I did but it didn't take me two minutes."

Peter;

"Peter, why did you deny the fact that you had an argument with your father?"

"Because it is the truth"

"Is it also the truth that you was upset and used the word intestate a few times?"

"Who told you that?"

"Just answer the question."

"Yes, we may have discussed intestate in passing but I don't quite remember."

"You deliberately left your wallet in your room then sent your wife to fetch it as you poured out his tea and poisoned it."

"That's not true."

"I can prove it; I managed to get your fingerprints off that cup of tea. It was quite prominent."

"That proves nothing... But wait a minute, where did you get my fingerprints?"

"The drink we had together, remember."

"You are an idiot Holmes, and you can prove nothing because I am innocent."

"That's your opinion."

We finally got a confession out of Peter. He had planned the whole thing knowing that even if he made a mistake in the bush in Africa, nobody would notice. And he would have gotten away with it had some generous client not paid for me to be on holiday at that gaming lodge.

Watson still had a puzzled look on his face. "I thought you said you missed your lab and had no way of doing anything scientific? How did you get the fingerprints?"

"Improvisation, my dear Watson. Sticky tape and a little ink did just fine."

SHERLOCK HOLMES

The Case of the missing Mayan Codices

Awaking to bizarre aromas at 221-b Baker Street was never a novelty. In that early winter's morning in 1902, however, the pungency of a hideously foul smell that seeped through every crevice of my bedroom door was extreme by any standard. It made an attempt at continued slumber utterly futile. Still, under partial darkness, I reached for my robe without even bothering with my bedside lamp. I emerged from my bedroom to find Holmes cloaked in a leather apron, his face shielded with what appeared to be engineering goggles.

"Holmes, what the devil are you doing?"

As usual when he was involved in thought or experiment, my words went unperceived. I approached him to within a yard of where he was standing, I could not go any closer. The smell that emanated from a brackish liquid reposing in three trays that he had laid out on the table acted like a barrier that I could not cross. Finally sensing my proximity to him, Holmes veered his gaze toward me.

"Watson, excellent, I was in need of an additional pair of hands."

He proceeded to give me a pair of protective gloves -

"Put these on Watson." Knowing full well his nature, it was obvious that the most direct means to discover what he was engaged in was by assisting him with whatever was swimming in those ghastly liquids. He retrieved what in appearance, was a collection of rectangular pieces of fiber bound together with some sort of hardened lace. He placed a book on my gloved hands. "Take this to the basin over by the window Watson," he said to me in his instructive tone. I did as he asked and positioned the book into the basin filled with clean water. As I did this, I noticed that Holmes was busy moving two other similar books from one tray to another. When he finished he approached me over by the basin. "Yes, indeed," he uttered as he peered into it. He reached in with his hand and pulled out the little book. The water had rinsed the residual elements of the brackish liquid in which it had been soaking. As he began to open the fiber-like pages of this book I could see a smile form on his face.

"Watson, behold the secrets of the new world,"

Now that the little book had been properly rinsed, I was able to make out a series of hieroglyphic imagery appearing in a combination of rows and columns on each page. The whole thing did not seem to consist of more than forty of these pages. The style did not look like any hieroglyphic writing common to ancient Egypt or those found in the lands of Babylon. During my time in India and Afghanistan I had seen many ancient writing styles, yet this shared nothing in common with those.

"I didn't realize that you were interested in archaeological endeavors Holmes,"

"This is not some idle pursuit Watson," he responded rather curtly. Before I could modify my original statement, he continued, "idle dabbling in any discipline is for the mediocre of mind, you know me better than that. I use science and all that it can reveal as a tool."

Observing that I had offended his sensibilities, I attempted to soothe the air –

"I meant to say that an amateurish engagement can be a healthy way to cleanse the mind."

"Nonsense Watson, everything that one does should lead you to an answer which in turn will free you to address another question. That is what distinguishes a professional, such as I; from a leisurely minded hobbyist,"

"So what is all of this then?" I inquired.

"This Watson, rather these," turning his head to motion to the other two little books still resting in their brackish liquid, "are ancient Codices of Mesoamerican origin."

"How did you come by them?" I asked.

"They were brought to me late last night by Oswald Harrington. You are aware of him aren't you Watson?"

"Well, yes. Mr. Harrington is the fellow from the British Museum, is he not?"

"Correct"

It was not difficult to be familiar with Mr. Harrington in those days. After all, his name had been appearing in all of the newspapers for several days prior. As one of the curators for the British Museum, he was involved in accusations from misappropriation of artifacts related to a recent bequest to the museum from an anonymous donor.

"As I was saying Watson, these artifacts were brought here by Mr. Harrington shortly after you retired for the evening. He found them amongst his personal effects in the private study of his own home."

"Found them?"

"Yes, indeed," said Holmes continuing, "Mr. Harrington claims that he had never seen them before. They were seemingly left for him to find, or taking recent events into consideration, to compromise him further. Being the professional that he is, he immediately recognized them as being from the region of Southern Mexico and Central America. He dates them to a period several centuries prior to the arrival of the Spanish people in that land."

I suppose that I should have been accustomed by then to the fact that every day was a new adventure with Holmes, yet I admit that I felt a tad bit more intrigue than usual. After all, one does not stumble upon centuries old books from the Americas in your home by fault.

"When Mr. Harrington found them, they were covered in a thick layer of natural patina; primarily consisting of routine grime from centuries of accumulated soil and oils. In a way, it actually served to protect the contents. I devised a solution consisting mainly of sodium percarbonate to remove the patina without endangering the pages or inks used in the books."

"Amazing, very clever," was my response, accompanied with my usual and sincere admiration for the workings of his mind, "but why bring them to you?"

"Due to the accusations that Mr. Harrington currently faces, it is unwise for him to make use of the laboratory facilities at the British Museum. For that matter, it is unwise for him to be seen with any sort of unaccounted artifact anywhere. Having made my acquaintance when I assisted in bringing resolution to a sensitive matter for the museum a few years back, he felt that I was the logical choice to not only properly cleanse these invaluable items, but also to discover how they arrived to be in his study in the first place."

As he finished explaining to me how these books arrived to his hands, he proceeded to rinse the remaining two books. Similar to the first one, they both contained hieroglyphic writing laid down in a species of ink that was impressive for its bright coloration. The brilliance of the blues and warmness of the reds used in the imagery held a vibrancy that made it seem as if they were penned just days before as opposed to a length of time spanning centuries. As the last book was rinsing, Holmes said, "get yourself ready Watson, we have a reunion with Mr. Harrington scheduled for 8 o'clock this morning." In what seemed like a burst of energy, I prepared and dressed myself for the day. Having yet to eat breakfast and with the three ancient books safely in tow, he and I were soon in a Hackney en route to see Mr. Harrington.

Just prior to 8 o'clock, our cab pulled up to the residence of Mr. Harrington. Holmes instructed the cabdriver to wait. The cold air was clearly evident as could be seen with every breath of the horses. As those beasts exhaled, distinctive clouds of condensate would emanate from their nostrils. We did not approach via the front door. Instead, I followed Him as he headed straight for the service entrance. As we descended down the landing steps to approach the door, we found it to be open. We entered and saw a distinctive trail of crimson. Both Holmes and I recognized it instantly, it was blood. He turned back toward me -

"I do not suppose that you have brought your revolver with you Watson?"

I shook my head to indicate that my response was in the negative to his question. He turned his head forward again and led us through the kitchen, past several side pantries. As we cautiously inched forward, Holmes observed that the blood trail consisted of droplets of varying size.

"Whomever it came from, they must have been applying intermittent pressure on the wound as they walked. The lack of large accumulations equates this in all probability to a flesh wound." As he spoke those words, he increased our pace. "As such, whatever violent encounter occurred, the perpetrator is likely no longer here." As he finished that sentence, we climbed the service stairs leading to the dining room of the house. As we opened the door we saw Mr. Harrington sitting on a chair, leaning on the dining room table. I rushed to him; "Good heavens man! What happened?" Before Harrington could answer, Holmes intervened, "it is obvious what took place here. Mr. Harrington was undoubtedly waiting for our arrival in the kitchen as he had instructed me to enter by the service entrance to avoid unnecessary visual scrutiny. Prior to our arrival, another person came in through the service entrance. He was assaulted with a weapon, likely a short dagger no longer than three inches in length judging by the wound on his leg. This weapon was brought by the attacker explaining why no cutlery was disturbed in the kitchen itself. In all likelihood, the attacker had no direct intention to assault Mr. Harrington. A dagger of that size would serve you best in forcing the lock of a door, not in seriously injuring a person."

As I tended to Harrington's wound, Holmes words rang true as they always did. The wound consisted of a small puncture followed by a laceration three inches in length on his left thigh. Using some napkins that I retrieved from the dining room buffet, I bandaged his thigh and was confident that the bleeding had abated. Harrington, looking somewhat mesmerized by Holmes' deductions, said, "That is exactly what happened. I had sent the entire house staff, my cook, maid and valet to accompany my wife when she left for Paris to avoid all of the recent unpleasantness. I was alone in the kitchen awaiting your arrival when I heard some noise at the door. I thought that you had arrived fifteen minutes early. As I opened the door I encountered the startled face of a short, middle-aged man trying to force the lock." I continued to listen intently to Harrington while Holmes seemed distracted. He continued, "The fellow, in terms of girth, did not seem menacing at all. As I had said, he was smallish and dressed like a humble shopkeeper. When he saw me open the door in a single motion, he jammed the dagger into my thigh and fled. I walked up here intending to summon the constabulary station on the telephone device in the study, but paused briefly to properly assess my wound. That is when you two gentlemen found me."

Holmes disinterest in his oratory seemed to increase -

"Tell me Mr. Harrington, did this fellow speak to you at all? Did he utter any word or phrase during your encounter?"

"No; he did not say a word."

"I imagine that you did not hear any noise related to this fellow's approach, correct?"

"No, the first noise came from his footsteps as he approached the landing stairs, and of course when he was tinkering with the door lock." -

Holmes then jolted out of the room and traveled down the service stairs heading back toward the kitchen. I instructed Harrington to remain seated and I followed after Holmes. I caught up to him outside approximately ten yards from the landing stairs of the service entrance. He was looking down at the ground of the alleyway. He picked up what seemed to be some cigarette remains and brought them to his nose to actively smell. "Fresh, "they must of had been smoked no more than an hour ago; Most likely by Mr. Harrington's attacker." He then began to examine the cigarette paper. With that look in his eyes that always announced to me that the game is afoot, he excitedly said, "Watson, go to Harrington, summon whatever medical assistance he requires by engaging his telephone device. Tell him that he need not worry; he is no longer in physical danger. Do not be long; I will be waiting for you in the cab. Hurry, time is of the essence."

I did as he instructed. Harrington declined any doctor to be summoned. My own medical experience indicated that his wound was not serious. I moved him to a more comfortable chair in one of the sitting rooms and told him that we will return later to inform him of what had transpired. I echoed Holmes' words that he was no longer in danger. Nevertheless, I grabbed one of the fire pokers from the fireplace and left it by his chair as a precautionary weapon of defense. Once I rejoined Holmes in the cab, we were off.

He instructed our destination to be Victoria Station. Obviously, he had told the driver to dispense without any delay and as we were jostled about as he put the whip to the horses to gather a pace way too brisk to be considered safe for city traffic. As we arrived at Victoria Station, he rushed toward the platform of the departing train to Southampton. As I caught my breath from chasing after him, I noticed that he had engaged a tall, well dressed gentleman in a verbal exchange. As I neared, I could detect that the gentleman was speaking in a distinct German accent. By the enunciation pattern of his hard consonants, he seemed to be Prussian. After all of my time with Holmes, accent recognition became an assumed skill on my part. Due to the intensity of the verbal exchange, a commotion started to develop on the train platform. Two constables approached him, to whom he addressed by saying, "detain this man and search his baggage!" The constables at first seemed perplexed by what they were witnessing. I came closer, "This gentleman is Sherlock Holmes, renowned sleuth, do as he says please." While few people were able to recognize Holmes by appearance, experience taught me that, especially in London, nearly all within the constabulary recognized his name.

When the constables began to search the leather satchel that this German gentleman was carrying on his person, eight books - of a similar vein as those that Holmes had introduced to me earlier at 221-B Baker Street - fell to the floor.

"Summon Inspector Wesley of Scotland Yard," he instructed the constables, "have him interrogate this man, tell him those artifacts on his person are part of the Mayan codices that have undoubtedly gone missing from the Saxony Library in Dresden. Treat those artifacts with care gentlemen; they are quite old and immensely valuable."

As we waited for the inspector's arrival, he revealed to me the intricacies of what I had just witnessed.

"You see Watson, Mr. Harrington is completely innocent of the charges that have been hinted at in the newspapers these past few days. The anonymous bequest to the British Museum came from an unidentified German family. It consisted of several artifacts of varied origin. The manifest that was submitted to the museum included an entry for eleven unspecified items.

"Isn't that unusual, to not properly label or classify museum pieces?" I asked.

"If it were to involve the transfer of items from one museum to another, yes, it would be odd. However my dear Watson, bear in mind that this was a bequest. As such, the itemized list was generated by the solicitor facilitating the transfer on behalf of the donating family. It is not unusual when artifacts are held in private hands for many pieces not to be properly identified as they would otherwise be by museum curators. Have you heard speak of the Dresden codices?"

"I confess, I am ignorant to what they are," I responded. Holmes proceeded to educate me, "they are part of a larger collection of ancient writings attributed to the ancient Mayan civilization. Under circumstances that remain mysterious to this day, the bulk of the surviving writings and teachings of that once great civilization came to be housed in Dresden sometime during the eighteenth century. It was long stipulated that they all had been accounted for and properly documented. It was, however, rumored that there were additional scripts, additional Codices that were being kept in private hands." As he continued, he lowered his voice - "it was said that if all of the Codices were to be placed together, they would reveal a wealth of information, including locations used to store the secret treasures of the Mayan kings."

As he uttered that phrase, I found myself being drawn in by the ancient complexity of the story. At that precise moment, he released one of his short, but sharp outbursts of braggadocios laughter and exclaimed, "Codices and treasure!" and continued laughing some more.

To be honest, I could not see where he was finding the

humor in the situation; however, having known him as long as I have, I knew it was best to remain silent and wait. I did not have to wait long, as he soon resumed by saying, "the man that we have detained here is Hans Elmendorff, the Kaisers' personal diplomatic envoy to the Mexican government. I had seen his name published in The Times as being on the passenger list for the S.S. Bladworth set to sail for Veracruz later today from Southampton."

"What is the significance of that?" I inquired.

"Our dear Mr. Harrington may be innocent of what public opinion and the press may be accusing him of, but in other matters he is as guilty as sin. He and Elmendorff are part of a larger conspiracy. The Mexican government has recently settled an uprising that they were experiencing in the southern portion of their dominion. After years of turmoil, the violence suddenly stopped; Do you know why that is so Watson?" I indicated to him that I did not. He continued, "The Mexican government reached a resolution with the leaders of the uprising by giving them the only thing that would soothe all of their other lamentations - the return of the ancient Codices of their ancestors - the Mayan Codices that we know better as the Dresden Codices. To obtain them, the Mexican government offered a large bounty in gold to the Kaiser's government. The tricky part was how to get them out of the country undetected. When Harrington came to me late last night I was certain that something was amiss, I just did not know what."

As the crowd boarding the train grew, we had to move ourselves out of the way before Holmes could continue. "As I soaked the books in my improvised solvent solution, the fumes being released became rather vile extremely fast. That was not the sort of reaction which one would expect when dissolving normal patina. No Watson, those books also had an outer coating of an unnatural substance. A form of protective outer varnishes that when reacting with the sodium percarbonate; released a cloud of noxious gas. It was so intense that I actually resorted to donning the protective gear that you found me in this morning. I trust that the odor wasn't too noticeable."

I purposefully withheld my comments regarding the foulness of the stench and allowed him to continue. "It was then that I realized what was afoot, the newspapers all stated that eleven items from the bequest manifest were unaccounted for; in the flat, we had three ancient Codices; in Dresden it is common knowledge that eight Codices reside. It was as clear as day!"

I was slow in seeing his logic in this case —

"What the devil does it all mean Holmes?"

"Oh my dear Watson, Harrington did not misappropriate anything. Those eleven missing unidentified pieces simply never arrived. They were listed on the manifest in order to clear all customs stations en route to London. Prior to being delivered to the museum those items were removed by Elmendorffs' associates. Harrington was truly out of the loop at first. Undoubtedly a few days after the initial uproar of the missing pieces came to be, Elmendorff approached Harrington. You see, Elmendorff needed something from Harrington, his expertise on the three previously unseen and unknown Codices. The very three that are in your bag now."

Upon hearing those words, I instinctively tightened my grip on my bag, as if the value of those little books kept growing with each word coming out of Holmes' mouth. He continued, "I am certain that when the inspector arrives he will confirm that the Dresden library has detected some inconsistencies with the eight Codices that they have on display. Namely, that they were recently replaced with well elaborated forgeries. The original eight Dresden Codices are those that we just recovered from Elmendorff."

"But why bring the other three to you last night?" I probed.

"They had not counted on what would be required to safely restore the three Codices that had been in hiding for so long. It was made even all the more difficult for them when Harrington came under suspicion. Hence; Harringtons' visitation last night"

With a wide grin on his face he continued. "They simply needed to retain the services of genius." Humility in his aptitude has never been a trait of Holmes.

"But what about Harringtons' attacker" I asked.

"That was Archie, one of my street urchins. He is a deaf mute. I had him shadow Harrington to canvas our arrival at the early morning reunion. The cigarette remained outside; they were Bremerias'; Archies' brand. Undoubtedly he saw it prudent to probe a bit more than he should have. Remind me to have some stern communication with him later. I assure you Watson, Archie is absolutely harmless."

"So; the German government created counterfeit copies of the Dresden Codices to sell the originals to Mexico. In addition they also managed to unearth three other Codices that had previously never been displayed in public. Harrington went from innocent victim in this plot, to an active conspirator. And all of this you have deduced and solved before breakfast."

As I finished saying those words the inspector could be seen approaching the platform. The look on his face when he locked eyes with Holmes indicated that Holmes had everything on the mark. In the end, Elmendorff, Harrington, and three other individuals that facilitated this act were arrested. The eight Dresden Codices were returned safely to the Dresden library, the other three it was reported, were repatriated to Mexico by diplomatic pouch by His Majesty's courier. Codices and treasure in deed.

SHERLOCK HOLMES

In Murders on the Voyage to India

"Twenty minutes to three" said Watson as he stuffed his Tiffany watch into his coat pocket. "Twenty minutes since you checked last my dear friend," I replied. "The journey to India is going to take forever if you keep checking your watch every few minutes, not to mention you will ruin the hinge again." It had never occurred to me the difficulty that will face my most loyal friend as we first embarked on our long term vacation in over five years. He was not particularly fond of ships, no matter the size, as he was quite a terrible swimmer and the prospect of sinking could put him in a fit. "Do you suppose we left the door unlocked Holmes", he asked. "Try to have some fun", I replied. "If not for your own health, than for mine; I'm quite sure we have locked up and there is nothing to worry about. Could you imagine the scandal facing Scotland Yard if they allowed burglars in to the home of 'London's most noteworthy citizens of the year 1903'? I was not entirely sure that I had, in fact, locked the door to the place, but it was too late to do anything about it. As I looked from the front of the steam liner 'Alexander Percival' I could see the lowest outline of the darkest land of our great Continent. That particular cape was notorious for having terrible weather, however, the ship was in fine condition and thus; far the clouds remained at bay. I excused myself from the presence of Watson, as I could tell by the rapidity of his breathing and the enlarged glands in his throat that there was a strong possibility that he was going to vomit. As if the old boy needed me around for that. I walked along the length of the ship, meeting a few of the fellow first class passengers. I remembered thinking while London is the finest city on the entire earth; the air out on the sea had a unique quality that made every breath a singular pleasure. I soon loaded my pipe and propped myself upon the railing, taking in the peculiar site of a large bird, an Albatross, I believe. They had flown close to the ship for a better part of an hour, flying high in to the sky then suddenly diving into the water, plucking up some prey, and then dropping the prey on deck in order to feast. As I watched this macabre scene over and over, I became increasingly aware of a presence near me. I turned sharply and found myself face to face with a terribly tall man, with several pock marks on his face and a swirl of black hair upon his head.

"Can I help you my good man?" I offered. The look of shock must have been apparent on my face, for I could see his brow furl with temper. "I was asked to invite you and Mr. Watson to the dining hall of Captain Ringhold", he said with an insidious smile and an exaggerated bow. "There is to be a dinner tonight for some of our more distinguished guests". He just about growled the final line to me. "Oh, very good then" I responded. "I shall inform my friend as soon as he is indisposed". No sooner as I mentioned him, Watson came around the corner to where I was standing. He was pale with sickness, and it was obvious that he had been indeed ill. He looked at the tall gruesome fellow as they passed one another, and he gave me a questioning look. "Large brute of a fellow, isn't he", asked Watson. "Indeed". He wanted us to come to the Captain's table for dinner this evening which means we had best go and prepare ourselves. Are you well enough for the seafood special?" I asked, while shooting him a sly look. He swallowed hard. "Quite". We dressed smartly and began our journey to the dinner that evening. We had to go up and down several levels of the large ship in order to reach the Captain's hall. When we finally found the corridor leading to the dining room, the hall suddenly turned from the blue steel that comprised the ship, in to a fine mahogany paneling. There was quite a gathering outside the hall, and the anticipation in the air was palpable. Among the other distinguished guests for the evening were the Skiffins', a young couple of which Mr. Skiffins' was a wealthy trader, the Captain's son's John and George, the industrialist's Mr. Palmer and Mr. Bagwell, and the lovely actress Evelyn Reed. I made small talk with Palmer and Bagwell; they were trying to start a steel industry in the southern part of the colony and stake future claims. When the large double doors of the dining hall were finally opened, I felt my stomach turn as the brutal man who had extended the invitation to Watson and myself, was the personal manservant of captain Ringhold.

We filed into the room, each of us falling under the glare of the brutal man. As the Skiffins' moved into the room, Mr. Richard Skiffins' attempted to give the man one pound for holding the door open. He looked at the money, then at Mr. Skiffins' and finally settled on looking down and in to the eyes of Mr. Skiffins'. "I don't want your money," He spat. Mr. Skiffins' withdrew his hand, his mouth agape. Another large man with broad shoulders and a full brown beard appeared in the doorway and looked for the cause of the holdup. It was Captain Ringhold himself. "Is there a problem here?" He rumbled. "I don't want his money", repeated the brutal man. The Captain glared at him and said, "Then you must not want my money either. You have just forfeited your wages for the evening!" "But Sir" He protested. "Would you like to make it two evenings Jock? Then away with you" The brutal man finally had a name, and it was certainly fitting.

The Captain apologized for the incident and ushered us in to chairs near the head of the table. I could hear Mr. Skiffins' appealing to his wife that he had not meant any offense by offering the man money. "Jock is an odd man" said Ringhold, but he is as loyal as they come and not bad when it comes to keeping men in line." "I would say so," quipped Mr. Skiffins' and the table erupted into laughter.

The dinner was remarkably good, and we soon settled in to the smoking cabin for dessert and some good conversation. Captain Ringhold went around the room introducing all of us to one another. As it turned out, the Skiffins' were moving to India for a few years to pick up on the prospective gold market.

"It is a new venture for me," remarked Mr. Skiffins', "but the success I had in London has made me restless, I need something new to work on to see if I can bring it any of my famous Skiffins' luck and charm." We all shared a good-natured laugh and went about introductions.

Watson appeared to have gotten over his illness and had

rejoined the conversation in time for the Captains introduction. "Here, we have Mr. Holmes and Mr. Watson as some of you may already know. They are quite famous in England, particularly London, for solving unsolvable crimes." Evelyn Reed seemed most interested in this revelation and asked us to relate some of our most particular solved crimes. Having a fully stocked pipe, and more brandy than I usually take, Watson and I obliged the group with tales of our latest mysteries. "Of course, all of these stories are quite often the victim of exaggeration in the newspapers" I explained. "Nonsense" interjected Ms. Reed "I have heard about your case at the Baskerville Estate. That was no small task; and Moriarty" " We have our moments," I said with a wink. I was beginning to show signs of inebriation. "So what is it that brings you aboard the ship?" asked Mrs. Skiffins'. Are you trailing a dastardly individual all the way to India?" her sarcasm and impatience were obvious and I could not help thinking that the stories had offended her in some great way. "Vacation actually," I replied. "I figured that it would be rather enjoyable to miss one British winter." The room erupted into polite laughter and a few "Here, heres". "I see" replied Mrs. Skiffins'. "Thank you for an enjoyable evening Captain Ringhold but I fear that I must soon retire so that I can be refreshed enough for tomorrow". "Dearest" started Mr. Skiffins'; "Now now Richard," she said, "I am perfectly capable of walking back to the room on my own." We stood as she left and resumed our conversation, hearing stories of Sons' latest excursions into the heart of Congo.

Later that evening, we said our goodbyes and departed amicably from one another. I steadied myself along the hall, while Watson steadied himself upon the opposite side, and we made our way back to our room. I flopped into my bed and dozed off to sleep. Thus far, it had been the most interesting vacation.

Murder; The word swirled around my head like a burgundy in my glass from the night before. Two syllables that I had heard time and time before. Murder; Watson and I had seen the worst of the worst. Often, it came down to two entirely different syllables, money. Murder, Watson, Holmes, money. I would not have to worry about money for some time, but murder. There was always murder. Murder; "Murder." The scream echoed down the hallway shaking me from my slumber and into the dim vision of the electric lights. Someone was banging on the door and Watson scrambled to open it. I was bleary- eyed, still feeling a bit desensitized when Evelyn Reed burst in to the door. Her hands were covered with odious red, and tears streaked across her reddened face. "There's been a murder!" She repeated. I snapped to attention, "Keep calm, my dear and show me where it has happened." Evelyn Reed led us around a corner and in to the opposite corner which was darker than the other halls by virtue of a few light bulbs that appeared to have burnt out. Several other occupants had opened their doors at the call of murder and now stood gaping at us as we rushed by them. The scene was grisly. The man lay face down in the hallway with a large wound at the back of his head, and the thick dark blood spreading around him.

"Evelyn, I need you to go back to my room and bring back my black handbag with gold monograms S.H. on it" I hurriedly begged. "It will have the tools I need". She quickly turned away and ran back to the cabin. I turned the man over and looked into the cold, empty gaze of Mr. Skiffins'. Watson and I met each other's gaze and shook our heads, such a young man and such a waste. "I should think that I must go and notify the Captain at once" Said Watson. I could tell that the grisly site was not helping his sea sickness. "Yes go my friend" I said. I needed to examine the body and the scene quickly before the sire was contaminated by the presence of others. Captain Ringhold soon appeared, followed by Evelyn Reed and Watson, and gasped at the site. "Never in all my years" Ringhold murmured. "Evelyn, dear, hand me the bag please," I commanded. Time is of the essence. I examined the body, careful not to disturb the scene too much. I checked his pockets and found them to be empty. As I sat and began to deduce, I had the impulse to screw the bulbs in again. They flickered back to life. Before I could mention my findings to the Captain, we were interrupted by the deafening scream of Mrs. Skiffins' as she came into the hall to mark the identity of her husband. She crashed to the floor as I had seen so many times before, sobbing and pulling her hair. Ms. Reed comforted her the very best that she could, but she soon broke away from her embrace and took off. "Let her go" I cautioned, "She needs to be alone right now."

The body was moved in to the lower decks and I found myself in the smoking room with the Captain, his lieutenant, and Watson. "Shall we anchor on the coast and seek the help of authorities?" I asked. "We are far from the coast, and even then we are not in friendly territory," Said Ringhold. "I would not risk the ship or the lives of the passengers to go on land. We will continue to India and keep Mr. Skiffins' in the freezer in the meantime as shameful as it is." "Indeed," I said. "Of course, but you do realize that you put more lives in danger by keeping them on board with a murderer?" "Yes," He replied gravely. "I am afraid that I must ask too much of you both Mr. Holmes and Mr. Watson. You must find the murderer and put an end to this madness before we reach India. Please be discreet, we cannot afford to let any more of the passengers know." Watson began to object, but settled back into his seat. "So much for our vacation; eh Holmes?" "I have already come to several conclusions regarding this murder," I said, "the body is still warm my dear fellow!"

exclaimed Ringhold. "Yes" I started. "First, Mr. Skiffins' was attacked from behind in the darkened corridor. Moreover, he was killed in a single blow. There were absolutely no defensive wounds on his hands or face. One strike killed him. What does that tell us my dear Watson?," "It must have taken an incredibly strong man to kill him, most likely a large man" "Precisely." The other occupants of the room looked on, interested: I continued, "The fact that the bulbs were purposely pulled out of the place tells me that the murderer knew that Mr. Skiffins' would come across this particular corridor. Also, it tells me that this individual knew how to unplug the bulbs as not to deactivate the entire hallway's fuses. Watson picked up "We believe that it had to be someone who worked on the ship before, a large man; an angry man who could kill a stranger with little provocation. Even over a few pounds, perhaps." The Captains eyes shot wide open and a look of furious anger settled over him. It was quite uneasy to see such a large man in such a rage. "Jock" He roared. "That scoundrel I will kill him myself. "Now Sir, be reasonable. We need proof before we can go barging in and making matters even worse." The Captain did not heed the advice and stormed off to the lower quarters, sending men flying to hug the corridors in order to avoid his rage. "Not aboard my ship, unthinkable." "I followed him the very best that I could, consoling the ship workers that were unwitting victims of their Captains fit. Finally, we reached the quarters of the brutal man, Jock. Ringhold began to slam on the door with his fist finally punching a panel loose, leaving a large gaping hole in the door. He reached in with his fist and pulled the door open from the inside. "I hope that you have made your peace, boy." He stomped into the room, gasped, and put his arms back behind him to stop our progress. I peered under one of his massive arms and saw the cause of his delay. On the floor, lay the tremendous body of Jock; face down with several large wounds on his back of his head. "Holmes," Said the Captain "I think we have encountered a problem with your brilliant theory." I backed out of the room, flustered. It had appeared to be so simple, so full of sense. The money was offered Jock, and Jock had his revenge. People have killed, and been killed for much less, I thought. I asked the Captain to leave the room, while Watson and I began our inspection.

"Several blows to the back of the head," I mumbled as I was thinking out loud. "Well we both know that it would take more than one to bring that big bully down now didn't we?" said Watson. He let out a wry smile. "Yes Indeed, interesting" I said. I looked about the room and saw nothing out of place. "This was not a robbery." "I thought the same," said Watson. I stepped over the body looking over his desk while Watson inspected his bunk. I scanned the rather bare room, looking over his bulky luggage and out of the port window.

"What have we here?" Watson excitedly said. He held up a piece of white paper with a few lines of words on them. "And what does it say?"

' TONIGHT. ROOM 317. FOR US.'

"Did you happen to catch Mr. Skiffins' room number, Holmes? " "317". "For us", he said - "I think we need to have a discussion with the Captain." He looked at me puzzled. "I think I have just found our killer. Go see that they are found and locked in a secure cabin immediately." Again, we met with the Captain in the smoking room. The killer was not going anywhere. "The killer has been here all along," I started; "Rather tricky, but as I always say, there is always a connection between money and murder." "Since when did you always say that Holmes?" asked Watson. "Never mind that," I said, "the point is that we have discovered the killer and I would like to explain to the Captain my theory before we go barging into another room." "Pardon me gentlemen," Said the Captain, "but could you please get on with it." "Yes, indeed, could someone kindly get our prisoner -? "

"Murder" The scream echoed down the mahogany hallway and all four of us let out a collective gasp. A seaman barged into the room, breathless, and declared that one of the watchmen has been found dead on his lookout post. Impossible, I thought. Watson and I deduced the identity of the murderer thoroughly and with great care. We rushed along the corridors, up the stairs, and on to the starboard deck. I climbed the outlook post and found the body of the watchman just as they said. His bald head made it easy to see where the blow had been struck, leaving a wound on the back of his head. His white uniform had been stained a sickly red. There was no room for another person to climb in to the watch post without being noticed. I looked above the watch post and saw nothing but blue skies and a lone bird high above. Behind me were the smokestacks from the steam engine as we chugged inexorably towards India. I only had one other night to solve the case before we were docked. How embarrassing would it be to have the Indian inspector's take on the case from us. Then the passengers would know and certainly the papers; the papers, the papers, always the papers. I climbed down the watch post and sent the crewmen up to retrieve the man's body, all the while imagining how the press was going to treat Watson and I. I promised my friend a vacation, and now it had been tarnished by three murders in less than a day. Feeling a tremendous swell of self-pity, I took Watson by the arm and walked to the rail. "My dear friend, I am so sorry that this has happened. This was supposed to be a break from all the hardships that we have faced lately, and instead, we have more murders." I trailed off and I could see that Watson was uncomfortable. The injury that he had suffered on the last case still pained my friend. I could not afford to lose him as a friend or as a partner. "Holmes, you are my closest friend, we have worked together for many years. We both should have known that we were not able to take a vacation without complications". We chuckled and leaned against the railings. "I thought we had the killer," I said. "I just can't connect the last murder with the other two." I pulled out my pipe, struck a match, and took a long draw. "This is most unusual, Holmes." We stood there on the railing for a few more minutes until we were interrupted by a sudden clatter on the deck. I turned quickly and found a hard, oval shaped object on the deck. I held it up to my face and uttered, "Ah, there it is." Watson looked at the object and began laughing. "There it is indeed."

I rushed into the Captain's smoking room where he was puffing away on a cigarette and wringing his hands together. The lieutenant was looking out of the window. "Please tell me you have found something," He said. "We will be ashore tomorrow and there are already rumors swirling." Watson brought in the recently widowed Mrs. Skiffins' and sat her down on the couch opposite the Captain. She was scowling. "My dear Captain," I exclaimed. "Everything is solved. All thanks to this." I handed him the hard object, he held it up to his eyes, frowned, and then placed it on the table. Four legs came out of the object and it stood up. "A turtle," He asked. "What is the meaning of this nonsense?" I sat down, puffed my pipe and began. "The first murder took place while we were at the dinner gathering. You sent Jock away to his room where he went and sulked, the only other person to leave the room was Mrs. Skiffins' here. She was supposed to go back to the room but she ran into our wonderful Mr. Jock. You see, she was on a trip to India with her husband where they would have stayed for the foreseeable future. However, she did not want to go to India, she wanted to remain in England. Given the weather, I do not know why that is the case, Nevertheless. So she talked to our Mr. Jock and made some promises regarding her person and her means of wealth. After all, the only thing between her and happiness was her husband. Mr. Jock saw to it that he would not be a problem. Watson, would you care to go on? I seem to have run out of tobacco." "Certainly; our man Mr. Jock, took this note." He held up the note that was found on Mr. Jocks' body.

'TONIGHT. ROOM 317. FOR US'.

Was it money that you offered him Mrs. Skiffins' or something else?" Watson raised an eyebrow and continued. "So Mr. Jock killed Mr. Skiffins' and left his body in the corridor to be found. After Evelyn Reed came to us and asked for our services, my friend Mr. Holmes examined the body until Mrs. Skiffins' came to identify him. It was a fine act Mrs. Skiffins', but all you wanted was to make sure that the deed had been done."

"And how do you know they were co-conspirators?" asked the lieutenant.

"It was rather simple actually, Jock was a loyal man. Not the type to leave the ship without notice, for sure. Yet in his room, every possession he owned was packed into two luggage containers, ready to depart when we docked in India. I remember thinking how absolutely bare it was for a man that lived aboard a ship for months at a time. Aside from a lovely young woman, nothing else could make you leave quite as fast as a possible murder conviction.

"I knew he was a devil." growled Ringhold.

Mrs. Skiffins' spit at Watson's feet. I resumed the tale. "So while we were in the smoking room coming to the conclusion that our devil was Jock, Mrs. Skiffins' went and covered her tracks. After all, she had the alibi that she needed. All she had to do was kill Mr. Jock and she would be free to inherit and return to England with all his money. The argument between the two men over one pound was enough to provoke a man like Jock. However, that leaves the small issue to what had happened to the one pound. It was not in Mr. Skiffins' pockets, nor was it in Jocks. Mrs. Skiffins', would you be so kind as to turn out your pockets.?" She pulled out a crumpled note and threw it in my face. "There we are. Taken from Jocks pocket I presume. After you smashed him in the back and killed him, of course. From that angle I see he must have let you in the room and then turned his back. Was he going to show you that he packed his bags like a good puppet? No matter, you killed the man. Devil or not, that is murder. That, my dear Captain Ringhold is the story of the two murders."

"Two murders;" He stammered. What about the third, why is this bloody turtle on my table?" He pounded his fist upon the table. I began again. "That was not a murder after all. You see, it made no sense for another murder to take place while we had the killer, unless we had another killer in our midst. However, the watch post is high up and there is no way to sneak up on a man in the turret. The only thing above you is open air. Open air, where an albatross will sometimes fly high above and drop its prey to the deck below to kill it, or in this case, to crack the shell. Our dear watchman was the victim of bad luck and having a bald head that resembled a rock." I picked up the turtle again; this here sea turtle is the culprit in the watch man's death, though I doubt that will hold up in court, as well as Mrs. Skiffins' murder conviction." The Captain and lieutenant looked dumbfounded, but quickly regained composure as the ships horn told us that we had ported in India. Mrs. Skiffins' ended up getting her wish of going back to London, but not quite in the fashion that she imagined. I hear that she was tried for both murders and found guilty thanks to a few correspondences that Watson and I had sent. The turtle was set free in the water off of the pier, and Watson and I disembarked and found ourselves immediately engaged by the press. We had our pictures taken and gave a few quotes as we wheeled our luggage to the end of the dock.

"Watson, old friend" I said. I think it is time that we get on with our vacation." "As do I Holmes.-"

At the end of the dock where the wooden boards turned into to a paved street was a little boy who held out an envelope with my name on it. I took it from him and before I could question him, he ran away. Inside the envelope was a single leaf of paper that read simply:

'Dear Mr. S. Holmes and Mr. Watson, welcome to India, I will be seeing you soon.

Sincere regards,

M.

SHERLOCK HOLMES

In The Heist

I had paid a call to my friend Mr. Sherlock Holmes one evening the spring of last year, and discovered him pacing about his parlor, stepping over his vestiges of the several experiments that he had been conducting over the last months. While a few of them doubtless had come to completion, others still lay in the chaos of irresolution: a yellow powder lay on almost half the carpet, having spilled out of a beaker on the table. Holmes' footprints had brought this yellow substance all over the room; from the heavy traffic pattern, it was clear that he had been pacing for some time now. He barely looked over at me as I came in to the room, still walking and mumbling to himself. Setting my umbrella on the table, I greeted him, "Hello Holmes. What's all this about?" Holmes continued to pace for another minute or so, making three more circuits of the room then he looked over at me, his eyes wide as though he had just marked my presence. "I am working through, Watson, the most intriguing puzzle."

"Well, if you keep working through it, you'll have a carpet that is entirely yellow."

Looking down, Holmes started to chuckle, "Right so, Watson. I didn't even notice that had fallen over. "Peering at the mess, Holmes let out a low whistle. "I was examining the cleansing powders of Sulfur based on a memory I had from Homers' Odyssey. Remember at the end, when the brains and blood of the suitors of Penelope had created such a stench that Odysseus had to use Sulfur to get it out?"

"Of course Holmes, but the process required burning Sulfur. What on earth were you doing with it?"

"I was about to mix it in with a soap powder of my own concoction - here," my eyes drifted over to the table, where another beaker with white powder in it had not yet suffered the fate of its companion – "to get a particularly stubborn stain out of one of my best shirts."

"So you're pacing back and forth because of a laundry quandary?" I raised my eyebrow incredulously at him. Holmes glared at me with scorn; "Of course not," he snarled. "Lestrade just brought the newspaper by to get my opinion about this morning's headline. He thought I might know something about it."

Looking down at the paper on Holmes' clean desk (relatively speaking) I saw the words 'HENRY BANK & TRUST HIT' run across the top. I had heard about this recent crime at my supper club, so I already knew why Lestrade was feeling the need to consult his most reliable consulting detective.

"So what's with the pacing?" I was truly disturbed to see Holmes this agitated, because his usual state of contemplation involved sitting still, going through pipe after pipe until it was almost impossible to see across the rooms at Baker Street.

"The crime itself is simple in its inexplicability," Holmes said as he finally stopped and looked at me. "The robbers seemed to have disappeared without leaving the bank, and the bank lost no money or jewelry. Hostages were taken, but then they were all released. After all the hostages had come out, there were no robbers left inside the bank. The police searched all of the space within the bank, at least according to Lestrade."

I had heard about the hostage situation, but had not heard that the bank's assets had emerged unscathed.

"So what is the crime, Holmes? Why is Lestrade even involved."

He was at a loss to tell me, even though I asked several times.

"Clearly there is more to this man than meets the eye. A representative of the bank is due to come by here ". He stopped to look at his watch – "at any minute. Will you stay to talk to him with me Watson?"

As I had no pressing engagements and was admittedly interested in the case, I agreed to stay and converse with the two of them, as long as Holmes agreed to get the yellow powder up. I rang for Mrs. Hudson, and amongst the three of us, we had the apartments in almost tidy shape when a knock came at the door down on the street. "That, no doubt, is the man. " Holmes averred. Mrs. Hudson scurried down the stairs to open the door, and soon the representative of the bank was in Holmes' sitting room. The representative, however, was no man. Instead, a young woman sat across from Holmes and I, having gingerly settled on the least dusty chair in the room. Her hair was a deep auburn and she wore a scarlet dress which came up to her neck settling on a lace collar. A matching scarlet hat sat atop her head, with a brown plume standing proudly upon it.

"Gentlemen, I am here to represent the interest of Henry Bank & Trust. We would like to resolve the situation quickly and quietly, so that all the investors can move forward with a minimum of anxiety."

Holmes sat across from her, studying her with a nonplussed air. "I must admit" he said, "that I do not know how to assist you. Inspector Lestrade was here earlier, and it appears that you are missing nothing and they have no thieves in custody. When the bank emptied today, everything was in place, except for the criminals."

The young woman smiled, "Perhaps we have started things too precipitously. My name is Geraldine Charlatane." At this, Holmes nodded, and closed his eyes with a slight smile. Before she noticed it though, Geraldine went on, "there are a few items missing, but they are only of value to the owner of the bank. We chose not to reveal this to the police because of their sensitive nature; However, I can assure you that the funds in the vault would have been a less costly loss to the Henry family."

"Might I enquire as to the nature of these items?" Holmes asked.

Geraldine smiled again. "You may, but I am not at liberty to reveal that information to you at this time. It may become necessary later. But Mr. Henry has elected to keep that a secret for now."

"Were the items taken from the vault? And has the bank also decided to keep the whereabouts of the thief a secret?"

The smile widened in to a chuckle. "No Mr. Holmes. We have not hidden the thieves anywhere. In fact, we are just as in the dark as the police on that matter."

"I see," Holmes said." So how may we be assistance to you?"

"We need to find the materials. If we get the items back, we are willing to forego criminal charges, so that this simply can pass in to the mists of time without any more publicity."

"Well, if we are not to know what you are looking for, that makes things much more difficult."

"We think that when you find the thief, you will find the items easily. They are small enough for one to conceal and carry on ones' person. The police searched each hostage from the bank thoroughly and did not find any of the items. Somewhere the thief must still have them."

"Very well, Miss Charlatane, I would like to tour the bank."

"Of course Mr. Holmes, we can head there now, if that suits

your schedule."

"Absolutely, also, I must spend a few minutes' time with Mr. Henry."

"I'm not certain—"

"Miss Charlatane, you are not just asking me to find a needle in a haystack. You are asking me to find an unidentified object, which may be invisible inside an ocean at this point. All I need is at most ten minutes' time with Mr. Henry. Can this be arranged while we are at the bank?"

"Miss Charlatane flushed for a second. "Yes Mr. Holmes. That will be fine."

"Very well then, Watson, shall we?"

A few minutes later, we found the three of us in a Hansom headed towards Henrys' bank. Holmes said nothing, instead sitting with his attention rapt on something out of the window on his side of the cab. This left me to sit and make pleasantries with the young Miss Charlatane. "So, how did you become the representative of the interests of Henrys'?" I inquired.

Her eyes opened into limpid green pools as she talked, or at least they appeared to. I felt my wedding band tighten on my finger (although of course an alienist would not agree with me), reminding me of my own beautiful wife.

"My father was a long associate of Mr. Henrys'. I grew up walking the halls of the bank, as my own mother passed away in childbirth. I grew up in the bank, learning of all its secrets and earning the trust of Mr. Henry. I realize that I am likely the only woman with this sort of position in the entire city, but I am in charge of making problems go away. I have a fairly impressive track record in doing so." She finished, giving me a meaningful stare. Holmes now turned to gaze at Miss Charlatane. "Really," he uttered; "and what sort of problems have you made go away?"

"All the ones you haven't read about in the paper, of course. "She rejoined. "That's how I get my job done."

"This story," Holmes replied with a quizzical glance, "has already made it in to the paper, so you have failed in this instance?"

"You won't read about it again," she grinned at him. "With your help, we will get to the bottom of this, and find the appropriate solution."

Holmes looked back out of the window, and none of us spoke again until we pulled up to the bank. Henrys' Bank & Trust was not one of the grandest banks in the city but those in the know were aware of the vast wealth of this unassuming facade and how it was represented. We entered the bank through the front door, and to all appearances things appeared normal. There was a queue of customers, and tellers were at their posts behind the counters. "This is not your typical crime scene," I murmured in Holmes' ear. He whispered back, "Well, according to Lestrade, there's no crime, at least, not yet."

"Mr. Holmes", a voice boomed to our left. We turned to see a tall white haired man, solid in build but not run to fat, which was impressive for a bank president in his sixties. We assumed that this was the man we had come to see.

"Mr. Henry, I presume," said Holmes.

"Indeed," he answered, "but I am not the man you want to talk to. I have turned over active management and bank activities to my son; he is ready to meet with you now."

Holmes walked over to the elder Mr. Henry. "Of course Mr. Henry, but may I inquire if you have recently been to China?"

Mr. Henry looked at Holmes confused. "Well, yes I have, Mr. Holmes. But how on earth did you know that?"

"The same way it is apparent that you have spent some time in prayer for a loved one today, and that retirement is not a pursuit to which you have resigned yourself completely yet."

Mr. Henry smiled ruefully. "True enough, but how could you tell all of those things?"

"Simply by using my powers of observation; the green tattoo that protrudes from your left sleeve is made from an ink that is only available in Chinese tattoo parlors. Your right cuff betrays a couple of drops of wax, indicated of having lighted a candle in a church and then holding it for just too long of a time that the wax runs down and ends up staying on the clothes, at least a few drops. Finally, you have looked at your son's office door for no fewer than ten times in the course of our brief conversation that tells me that, in a way, you still consider it your office and so retirement is still a new experience for you."

Mr. Henry chuckled. "Very clever Mr. Holmes, I am impressed. Let us go now, and I will introduce you to my son."

"Very well, Mr. Henry," Holmes answered. "Are you missing anything as a result of this incident?"

Mr. Henry's face became very serious. "We are, Mr. Holmes. We are. Let's go and sit down with my son."

Sitting in the office with the bank president was a very intimidating experience, with skins of wolves and even a brown bear decorating the walls along with several stuffed heads and skins. On one wall was a small collection of Chinese tapestries, and it was to these that Holmes turned his attention. Before he could examine them thoroughly though, the younger Mr. Henry spoke up. "What can I do for you gentlemen?" He asked. Holmes turned his gaze to the young Mr. Henry.

"To be honest, I am not sure what we are looking for. We were hoping that you could help us."

"Very well Mr. Holmes. There are some items that have been taken that could ruin the position of the Henry family in London and in British finance. We need to find him. The identity of the thief is immaterial."

"I see. May we begin the tour of the bank?"

"Absolutely, but first, let me tell you what happened. "

Holmes nodded once.

"Yesterday morning at about twenty minutes after nine, two men came in to the bank wearing black trousers and hooded coats, along with black masks that had holes cut out for the eyes, nose, and mouths, from a fabric. One man pulled out a pistol and fired it up at the ceiling. As you can imagine, there was some screaming, and the men ordered the customers, tellers, and manager to get onto the floor. There was an off duty bobby in the lobby as well, and he joined the rest of the crowd on the tiles. The other man used a chain to lock the doors within after first putting a notice on the door that hostages were inside. "

"Quite an unusual notice, to be sure; "Holmes murmured.

"Quite, it took more than an hour for the police to be summoned and to arrive. At some point, the men handed out identical trousers, coats, and masks, for the hostages to put on, ordering the hostages to take off their own clothes and put these new outfits on. One of the criminals stood at the door and apparently told the police officer that they had enough ammunition to kill all of the hostages before the police could force their way in. Then, he locked the door again, and no one came out for the next six hours."

"Incredible, "Holmes said, even though he had heard all of this from lestrade. "And then what happened?"

"The door opened, and two children came out although they were still wearing their own clothes. Then an elderly woman whom was coughing badly came out. She was wearing the strange black outfit. Apparently, she had started coughing inside the bank, and even water had not helped so they had sent her out into the street, locking the door quickly behind the three former hostages. It was through talking to these three hostages that the police put together what had happened up to that point."

"Indeed, and then -"

At the stroke of midnight, the bank doors opened, and twenty six people came out of the door all in these black outfits. Some officers came up to take these people into the hall across the street for debriefing, while a couple of employees ran back into the bank to accost the robbers. Inside, though, they found that the vault was open – but still full. It was only that we knew what to look for that we knew that our most important asset was missing."

"An asset that you still refuse to identify?"

"For the moment, yes. But you can investigate the crates we found."

"Crates?"

"Yes Mr. Holmes. There were two crates. One held several more black outfits, and the other simply held some powder at the bottom. They are in our conference suit. I can take you there now."

"Please lead the way."

The younger Mr. Henry lead us out of his office, across the main lobby of the bank, and in to a large room. Each of the crates were four feet high, two feet wide, and six feet long.

"When were these crates brought in?"

"None of the hostages could tell us that precisely. They only knew that they were there when it was time to change clothes, because the outfits came out of them."

Holmes looked quickly in to the crate with the extra outfits, I peered in there as well and other than the outfits, we saw nothing else. When Holmes leaned so far in to the other crate that he almost fell in, I grabbed his hips and steadied him before peering in as well. A fine grey powder lined the inside of the bottom of the crate. Holmes pulled his hand out with some powder on it rubbing it between his fingers.

Looking up, Holmes asked, "Are there deposit boxes here?" after the younger Mr. Henry nodded, Holmes said, "I would like to see the room where they are kept." Mr. Henry closed his eyes and then nodded again.

We all went in to a room filled with boxes on the wall each with a number. Holmes looked up and down the walls, his gaze stopping at the box between the number 391 and 393. The label on this box was blank.

"Mr. Henry," Holmes asked. "What is the purpose of this box?"

"Mr. Henry swallowed, and then he said, "I do not know."

"The president of the bank does not know the purpose of a deposit box without a number? Intriguing; should we bring your father in to ask him?"

"No need" That booming voice again came from the doorway. That's my box 392. And it's empty. That's what the thief came for."

Young Mr. Henrys' head snapped up. "You mean -"

"Yes, that's what I mean. Mr. Holmes, you are looking for items that would fit in to that box, and one can easily carry."

"Very well," said Holmes. "Now, I would like to tour the entire back area of the bank."

And so we went through the vault, and Holmes paced through every inch of it checking out the shelves, and the walls. Then, he opened an adjacent closet and walked into it. I came up behind him to see him pacing in the closet, then back out the door. He then proceeded to count to himself: presently, he came back out and looked to be counting his steps into the vault, all the way to the back wall. After a few minutes in the vault, Holmes came back out.

"Gentlemen," he said, "now we wait." We made our way back to the bank lobby.

"Is this the only entrance and exit to the bank?"

"Yes." The younger Mr. Henry said.

"And the rear of the bank?"

"Granite, just like the rest of the building."

"Well then," Holmes said. "Let's sit down. Watson, do you have your pistol with you?" I replied in the affirmative.

"The criminal is going to try and walk right by us. Keep everything going as normal."

The older Mr. Henry looked at Holmes as though he was insane. "How do you know?"

Holmes just smiled. For the rest of that day, customers came in, conducted their business and then exited their way back out. As closing time got closer, and the bank filled up with customers, Holmes stood up, keeping his eye on the back of the bank. I followed his gaze, but saw nothing untoward.

A well-dressed Asian man turned from near one of the teller counters and made his way toward the exit – and toward us. Holmes nudged me, and then he stepped forward. The Asian man was wearing a Western suit with impeccable tailoring and was carrying a brown valise.

"Excuse me sir." Holmes said. "May I assist you with your valise?" Before the man could react, I had taken it out of his grasp.

"That is my property, Sir", the man said. "Please return it."

"Of course," I said. "As soon as Mr. Henry has a chance to have a look at it."

The man was about to break into a run, but a swift movement from Holmes' cane left him sprawling on the floor. I opened the valise, and found a pouch. Inside were some diamonds, rubies, and other assorted gems. There was also a document written in Chinese. The off-duty bobby came and put the man under arrest. The older Mr. Henry came and took the packet from me. "Thank you Sir, you have recovered my property, but how did he get this?"

Holmes beckoned to us. "Let us take a look in the closet next to the vault. I believe that we will find that some of the wall has been disturbed."

Sure enough, a block in the bottom of the wall had been pushed out.

"I discovered that this room was smaller than it should be, about four feet too short. The grey powder was consistent with that of stone blocks that had been milled to resemble the blocks on the interior walls. While the hostages were busy in the lobby, our master thief was making a secret hideout for himself, right in the bank. When the time was right, he walked right out of the front door."

I asked." But how did you know he was Asian."

"The older Mr. Henrys' tattoo was Chinese in origin, and the color of the ink first became popular their during the Boxer rebellion. If we had asked, we probably would have found out that Mr. Henry served in the British regiments that prevailed at the battle of Peking. This battle was notorious for the looting that took place afterwards. While they broke no British laws, the looters came out with a lot of treasure from homes throughout Peking. I'm sure the police will discover that our thief simply came back to get what he thinks it to be his family's rightful property. And now, Watson, perhaps we can get home for some of Mrs. Hudson's chops. I believe it is the right day for them."

SHERLOCK HOLMES

The Game of Cat and Mouse

Today seems to me particularly vile in nature with skies as grey, grungy and tattered as the laundry around the lower flats. Such a day invites little in the way of neither comfort nor mental peace, but seated by the fire with a more than serviceable cuppa, I should be restive if not entranced by the flames. Sadly the whining of Holmes' current solicitor refuses to be ignored. A large, lurking specimen with hair fit to shame even a hedgehog and the voice of an unoiled crank he persists in rambling on. With his strangely bright dish water blue eyes and a disquieting aura of energy he brings to mind another solicitor - one who honestly is hard to forget. And it would be a lie to say that I have not tried my level best to do so these many years.

It would have been some three years ago when a certain Mister Creed wandered through the door. I can recall I was not of mind to deal with anyone that day as it marked two years since my dear darling Mary left this benighted earth. Damned if Holmes was not aware being not only the most frightfully intelligent man I have ever known, but one who never left slip the slightest bit of information. Besides which he had stood beside me as they lowered her, hadn't he? But I digress as I am wont to these days. Still he had called me to be present as a long time correspondent was coming in to finalize an agreement.

The time had been set for half past seven and already it was a quarter past. Holmes sat in his mouse grey dressing robe looking remarkably like a wax figure set to melt as he idly flicked through some tome or another. I will admit to being pettish as I said, "And what is it today Holmes? The seven percent solution again or have you decided to research the Lotus? We know how "lousy" you are with botany." Barely bothering to look up Holmes might have smiled, but clearly his attention was elsewhere. Still he answered saying, "I realize I have gambled rather heavily on your loyalty versus your grief regarding today, but I ask that you have some faith in my recognition of necessity." And as I sit here now I still cannot think what I could have said to such a reasonable request. It didn't matter either way as Holmes stood up and headed to his bookcase.

At that moment a series of knocks began battering the door. I thought to handle it, but even as I gathered up the energy, Mrs. Hudson was clacking toward the disturbance. Well, not a disturbance as much as what was a rather robust rendition of "Old Dan Tucker". Abruptly it stopped as the dear woman yanked open the door. There was then an awkward pause as though the poor lady was unsure whether she trusted whoever stood there to come in. That of course did not speak well of the visitor as by that point Mrs. Hudson was rather use to all sorts coming through from Princes to the Baker street Irregulars. Another moment and then I was treated as to the reason for the dear lady's hesitation.

Mr. Creed might well have been a tiger on its hind legs for all he resembled the average man. Brown as a nut he was broad of shoulder with a posture as straight as a breech tree. He was near as tall as one as well standing even over Holmes who was by no means short. His hair was cropped close enough that he might as well have been bald, though what remained was a dusty dun like that of desert dunes. That was not what arrested one's attention however. Creed was almost unnaturally handsome in a way that belied any attempt at guessing his race besides rejecting the idea he might be of African descent. His great eyes seemed to glow with a peculiar force as though behind them hid a furnace stoked high; coupled with his stature it left one feeling rather like a rabbit in the presence of a cheerfully bemused serpent.

A perfect smile shone forth before he spoke, "Good evening gentlemen. Might I trouble you for a sip of something? Perhaps brandy or rum if you have it" I was not expecting the pellucid quality of his voice or the sense of timidity it seemed to hold. Holmes on the other hand was bringing out a bottle of something dark and heavy as blood. There was again that same quality of smiling and not smiling that I had spied before. Pouring a fair measure of it into a glass at hand Holmes said, "I do not generally drink, but this was given me recently by a satisfied client. Might you like some? He assured me it was the very best." Cold as he can be let none say Holmes lacks a glib touch when the situation warrens it, for soon enough he had Creed seated with a glass in his hand and that strange energy subdued.

It could not have been more than a minute of waiting, but it felt certainly like years as the towheaded man drunk his glass down like water. In the meanwhile I studied his kit and wandered at its styling. Nearly white in nature it seemed to be of a heavy cloth except where it was brown leather. What was neither white nor brown was a bright red like freshly split blood. The manner in which it was made brought to mind some odd mix of court wear and noble savage. Why it should matter I could not have said. But something about his clothing put me on guard, for I felt as though I knew it from somewhere in my travels. Before I could grasp the thread of thought just out of touch Holmes began his meeting.

"Well-met Sir Creed - I had not ever thought to meet you in person. Over ten years of correspondence and only now have we finally met? Tell me Creed - why now?" spoken by Holmes as he reached for his golden snuff box. And here that menacing aura roused it's self again as the uncanny gentleman poured out a story of midnight chases, near escapes, and bloody horrors. Apparently Mr. Creed was an investigator in his own right following after a cult of individuals practicing a blasphemous faith that encouraged all manner of crime and assassination. Just recently he'd come across a tip regarding one of the head leaders - a Mr. House - and a particular piece of evidence in his keeping. He mentioned the evidence was unique as it appeared to be an Apple crafted out of solid gold. If Creed could but get a hold of it, he could take down the entire organization and bring justice to hundreds of cold cases.

When he finished, the poor man bowed his head in wait like a defendant before a "hanging" judge. Holmes meanwhile studied him as his long, pale fingers played with a certain black pearl. Yet again that flicker of a smile as Holmes asked, "And you can't go to the proper police for this?" There came a sharp laugh like the breaking of a bough or the snapping of a bone. A grimace that might have been a smile followed by another of those awful laughs; Passing his hand over a suddenly pale face, Creed said, "If only I could - but these are rich and powerful men. Tangled about their fingers are the leads to kings, presidents, generals, and priests. If I went public now it would only serve to see me dead." Again that strange unsmiling crosses my old friend's face and then he says, "Alright, I'm bored to tears as it is. Give me until next Friday and I will see that this... "Apple" is no longer in their hands. Good night." Creed was at least smart enough to know when he was being dismissed, which is more than most people can say. I don't know if I actually took notice of his leaving, so preoccupied was I with Holmes and that ephemeral smile.

I didn't sleep as well as I might have that night, and so was not particularly happy to discover Holmes gone for the day. As there was no help for it I thought to visit the city library until evening when hopefully he'd be back. I knew that I had seen something very similar to Creed's outfit somewhere before and I intended to find out where.

Perhaps I would have and thereby given myself a bit of a leg up for once in regards to Holmes, but it wasn't meant to be. Not long after leaving Mrs. Hudson's place a pair of gentlemen passing themselves off as Scotland Yard's best began to follow me. Oh, they were good - but prolonged exposure to some of the best has left me rather harder to fool than others. Fleet of foot I might be, but something told me that wouldn't save me if I attempted to run. Besides which there was nothing stopping them from waiting for me to return to Baker Street.

It was therefore my good fortune to spot young Wiggins smoking a cigarette as he leaned against a stoop crowd watching. One good whistle had him over to me and with a shilling or two in hand he ran off. Not even five minutes later my followers were shouting rather ungentlemanly terms as they danced about slapping themselves. I still don't know what Wiggins did and I feel the better for not knowing. I quickly made myself scarce by ordering a hansom cab and setting off to visit a friend of limited acquaintance who might know what I needed. His name doesn't particularly matter - for the sake of this story let's call him R. It was while in the army that I met R. a man with a rather singular interest in groups of a certain nature - for instance the famed Knights Templar. In the course of this he had amassed an unparalleled store of esoteric yore. Outside of the library he'd be my best bet.

Imagine my surprise to have his door opened by Holmes. Dressed in the attire of a low paid clerk and with it a pair of secondhand glasses on his nose I might not have known him, but for the cold brilliance of his eyes. If he'd of been a mind to I still might not have, but apparently he was hot on a lead. This proved to be correct when he said, "I had wondered when you'd get here my dear Watson." With that non sequitur, he turned around and wandered away into the rather gloomy murk of the hallway. Shutting the door behind me I followed him with something like frustration nipping at me. How in the devil had Holmes beaten me here? Furthermore; why would he? But at that point I had long come to terms with the impossible man outstripping me by miles in the department of deduction. If nothing else at least I could take solace in knowing I was apparently on the right track.

Walking into R.'s library was like stepping into a museum of dubious quality. There were pictures of men in armor beside weapons brown with ancient blood and everywhere stacks of paper, books, and manuscripts. In the midst of it was R. still whippet thin, but nearly bald with what remained was white as pure snow. Dressed in nothing more than his shirt sleeves and a pair of much patched pants he cut a rather eccentric figure there as he murmured to himself. As I walked closer I was able to see that what he was studying was a map, upon which were a mess of pins and makeshift markers. To the side laid a mound of letters and holding them down was an open book. I could not read the handwriting as languages were never of much interest to me, but the picture struck me like a fist to the gut. A man in white and red holding a weapon in each hand; and at his feet laid a man in armor perhaps a knight.

Looking to my right I was not surprised to see Holmes studying my reaction with all the concern of a cat carefully ignoring a mouse from the corner of its eye. "Rather familiar isn't it?" I said with what I hoped was a grin. Holmes merely nodded as though checking off something mentally and then turned back to the map. "R. was recommended to me some years back by a former classmate regarding the classification of certain artifacts." R. nodded with a wide grin as he tossed the letter in his hand on to the table which placed a domino atop some city or other. I had rather forgotten why R. was of limited acquaintance, but the words he spoke next reminded me.

"It was a dagger wasn't it? Very old, I've only seen one like it in my days and then only on sufferance. But I might see something like it soon, yes? Something very much like it"

And R.s' face pulled into a rictus someone more charitable might call a grin. One of Macbeth's crones could not have sounded so mad and foe in nature. I might have upset R then if Holmes had not distracted me with a question;

"Can you recall what the people who chased you looked like Watson?"

There must have been something about the look of my face because Holmes hummed and then said, "You've only just regained your color implying that previously you'd had a sustained period of stress or shock. Considering both your specialty and you're previous occupation that would imply that the situation was dire as in "life or death". That you frequently looked over your shoulder as you climbed the stairs tells me you expected someone to have followed you. Would I be correct?" Of course he was, but it did pain me a bit to admit it. Still I answered his request, "One of them was as tall and lean as a lamp post with hair as orange as a carrot and skin like skimmed milk. The other was average in every way except for his right hand which gave a violent twitch several times a minute. I paid Wiggins to distract them while I got away." Holmes nodded as a schoolmaster might at a fair recital.

"That explains why it took you so long to pay your fare. I hope you haven't overpaid him as I shouldn't like to renegotiate my terms with him."

I needed the laugh that prompted, not least because of the reason for us being there. Apparently Mr. Creed had his own organization he belonged to - an order of trained killers who were tied to dozens of murders across the globe. Mr. Creed himself may well have over two dozen to his name if the markers on the map held true.

"But what does this mean for the investigation? Will we be involving the Yard?" I asked earnestly. And never have I so dearly wanted to turn over a case to those fine fellows as right now, but of course Holmes demurred such a suggestion.

"But why" I asked. Surely you don't think -" But Holmes merely shook his head and I knew to accept that he would explain his reasoning in time. In the meanwhile a cockatrice of a hunt was on with someone hunting us, us hunting that blasted Apple, and Creed playing the wild card.

It was decided that neither of us would return to Baker Street, but would instead take lodgings elsewhere. In the morning Holmes would disguise himself and head toward the smoking club Mr. House frequented on Walters Street. I was slated to head back to Baker Street to see if I could catch my observers out. The hope was that I could perhaps trail them to their employer or else get close enough to glean some small bit of Intel as they idly chatted. Either way someone had to check-by to insure Mrs. Hudson had come to no harm in the meantime. The night passed well enough though I could not shake the feeling I was missing something desperately important.

At the crack of dawn I was up hoping to elude our watchers

by the dent of either the early hour or their own exhaustion. Not surprisingly, Holmes was already gone with his bed apparently slept in. With no note apparent, I figured he had simply stepped out to see about House and mayhap Creed. The streets were already beginning to buzz with life even as last night's dew arose in sheets of steam. Taking several back alleys, I made it to Mrs. Hudson's house with little difficulty and no sign of either the red-head, or the man-with-the-twitch.

With a perfunctory knock I brought forth my key and entered the boarding house. Mrs. Hudson seemed happy enough to see me, but there was a certain brittle quality to her smile. Clenching the dusty cloth in her hand, she said _"it's well enough you've come by Doctor, a couple of never-do-wells have been sulking around…one of them even had the nerve to come up and knock as if I was dim enough open the door."

And truer words could not be spoken; Mrs. Hudson, with all her tact, is as canny as any fox. Still, it was worrisome that they should be so bold as to actually come to the door. If desperation should strike them, they would likely attempt an actual break-in and that could well lead to dire consequences to the good lady. As such, I had thought to ring the yard and Holmes' but I'd be darned when their came a rapid rapping at the door. Sharing a look with Mrs. Hudson, I walked to the parlor and quickly found Holmes' seldom used pistol. I then approached the door, and with a mental count to three, yanked it open.

The little whelp on the doorstep regarded me with an expression that showed her rather less than impressed with my performance. That may have to do with the good five inches of space from the guns bore, and the top of her head. Either way, she simply held out her hand for payment while tapping one tiny boot-clad foot in impatience. With a sigh, I uncocked the pistol and reached in my pocket for a farthing to give her. After a quick bite to check authenticity, she handed over a rather filthy wad of paper. The time between the discharge of her duty and her disappearance was short enough to pass as magic.

"Well, what is it Doctor, it must be important if Holmes sent it along with one of them."

Her need to know was, and remains understandable but important as those situations may be, they tend to mean nothing good for anyone; so my hesitation I think, should not count against me. I thought that I should need a strong solution for my hands after handling the note. It seems strange to remember that thought so clearly, but I suppose the shock of what came next is what anchors it so well. A moment's pause, and then I found myself seated by the fire with a glass of cognac. Of course, there wasn't time to compose myself and with a second's regret, I tossed the drink in to the fire before standing.

"If you'll excuse me Madam, I need to meet Holmes at the scene of a crime – it seems my old friend and colleague R. has met an unfortunate accident."

Of course, having Rs' death occur under the current circumstances made the chances of this being an actual accident...pretty well, non-existent. The question therefore became who exactly was responsible – there were at least two possibilities that we know of... still there was no time to ponder the possibilities as I walked through a crowd of bystanders in to a maelstrom of activity. Holmes's stood speaking to one of Lestrades' lackey's as his eyes scanned over the gathered crowd. I waited until he spotted me and waved me forward to step amid the intricate steps of a full-fledged investigation. Holmes appeared pale, but unharmed – although I did wonder if he bothered to sleep after I turned in.

"My condolences Watson, it seems our association has led to his untimely demise." Waving off whatever the lackey – Duttwielder I believe – was about to say, Holmes led the way inside. The gloomy hallway blazed with specialty-made lamps as detectives that could have been human hound dogs crawled about looking for clues. It seemed doubtful that they would uncover anything considering how undisturbed the area appeared. Not a thing seemed out of place, and even the library appeared to be exactly the same – "Notice anything missing Watson?" Looking about, I see that our workstation from the day before appears altered... the letters and the books are gone as is the map.

"It seems whoever came through has an invested interest in our studies."

The quizzical look on my face must have given away my confusion –

"There is no sign of entry; true – however the position R.s' body was found in implies he was surprised by an aggressive attack. The injury sustained to head and forearms implies he faced a taller foe, but the lack of forced entry seems to indicate some level of trust. Rather a bit strange altogether. "

Allowing his words to trail off, Holmes' seems to be seeing something beyond my ken – abruptly he frowned and then gave a quick look around.

"I think we should go Watson – something tells me we are late for an appointment we dare not miss. "

Our exit was scarcely noted as we threaded through the rigmarole of the investigation and its attendant observation by the neighbors. Two streets over I saw myself walking along side what appeared to be a battered man bent nearly double with his years. It never ceases to amaze the change in perception caused by a certain walk or an adjustment in a person's posture – and Holmes has never been a master of these simple changes. The reason for this change quickly became apparent as I fell under the feeling of observation. A quick glance in the window of a shop displays the men from yesterday along with another gentleman who had the look of a photo out of focus. Grey hair blended with grey eyes and skin like fat gone rancid. Neither fat nor thin, the energy from this man was entirely absent. It was as though there stood a hole in the world where that man stood and I felt a sickness to my stomach that only seemed to grow.

From the corner of my eye, I saw Holmes make a quick signal as to fall back, and almost immediately he disappeared in to the morning London rush. The next few minutes were an agony of suspense and then I heard a querulous voice rise in argument with a harsh rumble that could only belong to a cab driver.

"Villain, Why not aim a shank at my kidneys while at it? Have you no respect for your elders? Cad! I have a mind to call over an officer of the law!"

"Law, why not; I'll even give you a reason when I break your fool head you old duffer!"

The racket is drawing enough attention that I am able to step out of sight down an alley. Not a minute later Holmes has me by the elbow and is leading me at a swift clip towards the Eastern end. There is a tilt to his lips that shows his enjoyment of the last few minutes.

"So you probably wondered where I got to this morning. Well I had planned on taking to my bed, but then I realized that some of my best contacts were likely to be just stirring at the time. This proved to be correct as I came across a gentleman of a particular type who happens to be a favorite of certain circles."

With a hard glance left and right, Holmes had us across the street and in to a Labyrinth of twilight and shadows. Several turns after that and I had no hope of finding my way back out alone. Another turn and we were blinking in the sudden brightness of day further down the Thames then I might have thought. Still blinking, I was relieved to find my arm returned to me albeit reluctantly.

"Keep an eye alight Watson this is a deeper game than we generally play. "

The great detective pulled forth his snuff box and took a pinch. After a sneeze in to his hanker chief, he focused on the grand glittering river with a frown.

"Earlier I trust you noticed your old friends in the company of a rather discording gentleman. That gentleman is the Mr. House we were originally supposed to be investigating and relieving of a certain artifact. Interestingly, my source states that Mr. House lives around this area."

Here he turned his cool gaze upon me with a resurgence of that not-quite smile.

"If you were looking to gather an artifact of any cost, wouldn't now be a perfect time Watson."

And it suddenly clicked – Creed was intentionally playing House against Holmes and Vise-Versa in order.

"By George" I said with a wince, "Were being had," A careful tilt of the head that may or may not have been a sign of agreement, and then a glance at the battered watch at the end of his fob.

"Another quarter hour just to be sure Watson and then I think we'll find something of interest over yonder."

I could have kicked myself for leaving my pipe and loose-leaf back at Baker Street but the minutes past by fast enough over all. Dumping out his pipe, Holmes stood and turned eastward. In a moment's time, it seemed we stood beside a grand old site. No lights shone forth, but for some reason, the house gave off a feeling of someone watching. Without hesitation Holmes passed through the open gate and up the stairs. The door opened with barely a touch.

"Coming Watson?"

With something of a huff, I followed behind him feeling for

the pistol at my waist and wondering if Holmes had his own in addition to his cane. Something told me that this case was likely to result in death or injury if we weren't careful.

The interior was dark and neither of us searched for a lamp or switch. There came a ticking of some clock or another. And the sound of a dripping faucet somewhere in the house was like a hammer to an anvil. Our breaths were loud, but my heart sounded louder to me. Interestingly enough, Holmes moved as though he'd been through here before. I had no time to ponder this as somewhere behind us, I heard a door shut and then the click of a lock. I slowly drew my pistol from its position and readied my thumb on the hammer. The whoosh of gas and then the darkness began to lighten. Still we continued until we came to what appeared to be a large library. Walls composed of varied texts rose uninterrupted from three walls while a set of leather furniture dominated the middle of the room. Display cases stood here and their offering forward curios and expensive bobbles. However, it was the person sprawled across a loveseat that unerringly drew my eyes. Mr. Creed gave an insolent smirk as his lilac pupils stared forward with something like hate.

"I expected you earlier Holmes, you wouldn't happen to be losing your edge would you?"

Rather than reply, Holmes merely walked in the room and

began to study the shelves. I walked to the other side glancing from Creed to the door and back again. There had been very few spots worse than this, but the calm manner in which Holmes continued to browse the selection gave me confidence. I will admit that watching Mr. House and his louts enter did nothing for said confidence.

Mr. House gave one glance around and then frowned – "Where is my golden apple gentlemen?" His voice was like the wind through the leaves – cold, dry and quiet. Holmes gave a shrug before checking his watch again.

"We have a few minutes, so if possible I'd like to keep this civil. If that is amendable to everyone present, then I should like to settle up accounts."

The redhead was about to open his mouth when a great racket came from downstairs. This was followed by a cacophony as voices and boots bounced off the walls and ceiling.

"Hm… apparently my watch is a bit slow… I shall have to see about winding it soon." With that observation, Holmes took a seat with a sigh.

The noise made its way up the stairs and emerged through the door with Lestrade at its head. With a singularly dour look Lestrade glanced around the room with a good pause before drawing his weapon.

"I suggest you make with the explanation immediately Holmes – I'm not in the mood for a drawn out presentation."

With one eyebrow quirked, Holmes turned first to Creed before beginning his recitation.

"The first thing that needs to be addressed is that the gentleman over yonder is not in fact Mr. Creed. Oh, are you startled. While I have no doubt you are an investigator – you are not my friend of past years. No Mr. Dewitt – oh are you very surprised? Did you think I wouldn't recognize a fraud?"

And here Holmes stands and begins to pace in a manner that might be called agitated in someone else.

"Ten years I and Mr. Creed have known each other, and for ten years, he has never been strident about vices – from opium to simple red wine. Never would he have asked for a 'tibble' – never mind swallowed it like water. Of course I would not have known to test you as I did have not you been so relaxed with your coding Dewitt. Despite his appearance, Creed was an orthodox Catholic, not a Muslim – your code however, failed to take that in to account when written. Still I might have missed this fact if not from aid from the man you killed – but, that was not the only thing of course. Creed was from the American Islands and his speech betrayed that fact. Meanwhile, you are obviously from the American South, a fact betrayed by both your love of the Minstrel "Old Dan Tucker", and your octoroon characteristics. To complete your mistake, you asked that we not involve the police, something Creed would have never agreed with. If it served to bring about justice, then that is what he wanted, even if it meant his death. Something you should have recalled all things considered."

Dewitt, had gone pale under his dark tan, but still he managed a hint of insolence as he pouted.

"Fine about pinning me as not Creed, but how'd you find out I was Dewitt?"

A genuine smile then – "Why your victim of course – he sent information on you, House, and several others, in the last few letters before you took his place. "

Dewitt at that point simply settled back and closed his eyes. "I guess I'll be waltzing Matilda then? Fine – but I shouldn't be swinging alone."

A nod in agreement and then Holmes turned his eyes on House who seemed only bored.

"Mr. House is, as R. could tell you, a member of a certain club that participates in a rather broad game. You are also a part of this game Mr. Dewitt and there by responsible for those deaths you were 'investigating' as House. The case in point being R.'s demise – both of you share responsibility for that. Dewitt gained an easy entry with his outfit and gear, but it was Houses' goons who took it too far. Would I be mistaken in thinking you arrived to remove certain bits of information Dewitt?"

"Sure – it was already gone though."

I saw a glimpse of bright blue eyes as Dewitt threw a glance at the detective. House merely yawned before he said, "even if you can prove Misters' Rook and Franks were at the scene – you cannot possibly prove I had anything to do with their –

"Abruptly, the older man cuts off as Holmes burnishes a rather dirty page –

"You might have warned your workers to be more careful of the whelps around Baker Street...as is I trust this to be your hand writing."

Handing off his evidence to Lestrade Holmes pauses before saying, "it's unfortunate that Creed had to stumble in to the midst of such an enterprise as you two are involved in. But then again, if he had not, who knows when you lot would have come to justice."

From there, it was the work of minutes to gather up the group and walk away. Holmes watched them all packed up in the van before walking in the opposite direction with a vague promise to turn over the relevant evidence concerning their crimes. It was quiet for a few minutes and then all of a sudden Holmes stopped and reached in to his pocket for something wrapped in cloth. A moment of contemplation and then with a casual toss he flung it in to the river beside us. I had thought to ask him what it was, and why he had done that, but I didn't need to, as he said – "What a stupid waste."

SHERLOCK HOLMES

Death in the Tropics of an English Explorer

As I was going through the many papers I had allowed to stack up in the rooms, I heard a distinctive banging on the front door. As Mrs. Hudson opened it to greet none other than the esteemed Mycroft Holmes, I could see the look on my roommates face turn from one of boredom to one of intrigue within a matter of moments. As Mrs. Hudson lead him upstairs, I opened our door and caught a glimpse of worry flash across his face, and I could tell that what he had come to discuss was something of great importance to him.

"Good evening my good lads, I see you are enjoying this fine day. Surely Holmes, you have better things on your plate than fiddling instruments and reading week old newspapers."

His attempt at small talk seemed to do little more than annoy the younger of the two siblings.

"Surely, Mycroft, you didn't come here to discuss the trivialities of our daily lives. You have a problem, and you need my help, so you might as well get straight to the point."

"Well, I suppose there is something you can assist me with my dear brother. A small matter concerning a crew under the instruction of the British government; they are exploring some of the furthest reaches of the British territories off the coast of western Africa, and they appear to have hit a bump in their plans. "

"And I suppose you expect me to solve the whole case on that information alone? Surely there is something more you can give me." Replied Holmes; quickly losing interest in the subject.

Mycroft continued, "Suppose I said that it is possible, while studying the lives of an indigenous tribe known as the Koburu, that the great explorer, Sir Hughes Blakefield, was murdered in cold blood, poisoned with his evening scotch. The most obvious theory would be that he was killed by the tribesmen, although no one knows how they were able to get the poison into his drink, or for what reason. From what

I've learned; they are a vile species who have been completely cut off from any sort of civilization and with no concept of the ways of the modern world. It seems apparent to me that this is the work of savages, case closed. Although we have no way of knowing how they did it; The only other people on the island being his loyal apprentice a fellow explorer as well as the cook.

Holmes intervened, "How do you propose I answer these questions with such a small amount of information? There are some things, which, even I am unable to deduce from just that."

From that, I could tell that Holmes' interest had been piqued, although he was not quite ready to bite as yet.

"The case and the information gathered about this tribe, is one of great importance to many people. If you are unable to come to a conclusion based on the information that I have given you, I ask that you make the journey there yourself, examine the work of Sir Hughes, and determine why a native tribe, with no knowledge of the outside world, would want him dead. "

An absurd suggestion, though I could see Holmes coming around to it.

"You can't be serious!" I blurted out. Not meaning to create such as outburst, but unable to contain myself any longer.

"You expect him to travel to Africa, alone, to investigate the death of one explorer?" Surely there are better things for the government to concern themselves with than this?"

"Well, I don't expect Holmes to travel to Africa alone. I have no doubts that you should go with him. And as I have said, this is of particular importance and must be seen too immediately. You both have been booked a passage on a vessel leaving in the early hours of the morning."

As we disembarked the ship, we were rewarded with a stench normally associated with the atmosphere of the tropics, and one that was most welcome after our long tiresome voyage. We were greeted by the late adventurers'

apprentice, a young fellow by the name of Gregory Rickman who was kind enough to show us to our sleeping quarters. After such a long and tedious journey, I was more than thrilled with the standard of accommodation we both were given, and looking forward to a well-deserved rest. Holmes, on the other hand, was eager to get started on the task at hand.

"If there was ever a time for rest my dear fellow, now is not it."

As he begun sorting through the various supplies we had brought along, I could see the wheels already turning at full capacity inside his head.

"I suppose we ought to begin with an investigation into the nefarious tribe we've been told about. It seems to be the obvious course of action, wouldn't you agree Watson? Did you notice on the way in, the statue adorning the entry way. Such an elaborate carving with so much detail and effort; Surely a gift of this sort should tell you that, not only did the Koburu not have any ill feelings toward our late friend, but that they were in fact, on incredibly friendly terms" said Holmes with an air of aloofness. "On top of that, Sir Hughes was poisoned while enjoying a pleasant evening safely within his quarters. From the information which we have so far gathered, how many of those tribesmen would dare to come so far inland to administer the lethal poison?."

"None, I should say. They are only known to venture away from their land only for hunting. Where then do you propose we begin our enquiries?" I asked, for no other obvious choice immediately jumped out at me.

"With one course of action ruled out from the beginning, I suggest that we should begin our examination with dinner. The only other people with access to Sir Hughes will all be sitting at one table. A brilliant opportunity to investigate work if I have ever seen one"

And with that, we made our way to the dinner quarters for what was sure to be an interesting meal. It was during dinner that we were introduced to the other members of the camp. The cook, a quiet man from a nearby island, who spoke not a word of our language, but had mastered the art of creating a sloppy mess of a meal that could almost resemble something edible. Then there was the elusive character of Timothy Bradford. A fellow anthropologist, whom had travelled to this remote island to visit his dear friend and colleague Sir Hughes, before the visit was cut short by his untimely demise. And finally, a chap called Gregory Rickman, the quiet fellow we had just met upon our arrival. With such a small cast of people to investigate, I was sure that Holmes would have this whole thing figured out by the end of our somewhat palatable feast.

Throughout the night, it became apparent to me that Holmes was surely wrong on this account. It was in no way plausible that anyone at our table could have been responsible for the death of Sir Hughes. The conversation was, all around, a pleasant one with our new companion, Bradford, engaging us with rowdy stories of his, and Sir Hughes' youthful adventures. Midway through the dinner conversation, perhaps, as a way to get the investigation started, I began my analysis into the events leading up to the poisoning.

"He was in good spirits throughout the evening, the drink was flowing quite smoothly and he had not a complaint in the world," claimed Bradford; between gulps of his own, stiff drink.

"So he didn't mention any concerns? No issues with any of the staff or tribesmen that may have kept him up at night?" I probed, trying to gain insight into the general perception about the murder of the man we were investigating. It seemed that the chap had been enjoying a pleasant evening in the company of his old friend and a fine bottle of old scotch.

"He sure did have a knack for story telling while the drink was flowing", - piped up Bradford. "Never have I met a man more enthralled by the minute details of the lives of indigenous tribes. There was nothing quite like listening to him tell the tails of his travels."

"And what did he have to say in his most recent foray into the heart of the Koburu?" I asked.

"Nothing as far as I know, but that they had an abundance of rituals completely unique to their life style. They celebrated even the most trivial of life events, with fervor saved for weddings and births in their culture. "

"So the evening was generally uneventful then?"

"Well it was, right up to the moment my dear friend choked down his last drink and fell to the floor." A look of grief flashed across his face at the memory of that moment. Any suspicion I may have held toward this man immediately vanished.

"And who had access to those drinks that could have administered such poison to him without tainting your drink?"

"A fair question my old boy! Why, it could have been anyone of us. I was with him throughout the entire evening and didn't see any foul play afoot. Of course, all of the bottles came from the kitchen, which is the cook's responsibility, and they were served by that quiet boy, where has he gotten too anyway? he seemed to be everywhere and nowhere at all, and the thought that there are only three suspects, myself included, whom continue to sleep under the same roof without knowing which one truly did it. Well, it makes me darn nervous every day to say the least."

He stated this, not trying to deny the fact; he too could be the guilty party.

"There seems to be no evidence among the people of this camp, as to who may have felt any ill will towards the man."

"Dear Watson, if the man had been at all disliked, we could close the book on this case quite easily. It occurs to me that there is something else going on here, apart from mere likability, and the answer is not among the people of this camp."

"What are you saying Holmes, that there is something to be found among the Koburu that may enlighten us as to the untimely death of Sir Hughes?" I asked; intrigued as I was under the impression that he had written off the possibility of the tribesmen having anything to do with his death. Perhaps he had come to the conclusion that his original assumption had been wrong.

"Do I think that he may have discovered something among the tribe that would be worth killing for? I should think that the answer to that be fairly obvious. I will be off tomorrow morning taking with me the Rickman boy; to see what there is to be uncovered in the village. Watson, I assume you will be able to hold down the fort until I return?"

"Do you mean to tell me that you do believe that the crime may have, in fact, been committed by someone outside of the village? Why else would you choose to leave your only suspects the opportunity to flee while you are off scampering through the jungle?"

I was becoming more enthralled with trying to untangle the reasoning behind my good friends' actions. For, it seemed that his words and his actions were completely contradictory of one another.

"My dear Watson, I will be doing no such thing, I am merely leaving you in charge of the camp while I gather the evidence needed to support my theory. No suspect shall be left unattended." And with those last words, he retired for the night.

As I awoke the next morning, it became immediately apparent that my dear friend had already left on his adventure for the day. While I had nothing better to do, I decided to spend my time getting to know more about the crew assembled in the camp. The chef spent a good portion of the morning unloading a shipment of supplies that had recently arrived. At which time I assumed that he made his way to the kitchen to make another futile attempt at cooking our evening supper. As I was unable to hold any decent conversation with the man, owing to his complete lack of knowledge of the English language, I decided to turn my attention towards Bradford. His general character was not of a murderer, hardly a murder master mind - so I didn't have much work to do. While it was possible that the motive for the murder lay somewhere among the tribe, I simply could not fathom any reason why this person would come to kill such an important friend and colleague. Money seemed the most obvious answer, as it was apparent that Sir Hughes' career was far more profitable than Bradfords', and certainly more profitable than the chef's, but if that were the case, surely there would be some sign of theft among the valuable possessions within the camp. This was obviously not the case, as all the statues and artifacts remained in their designated places, and none of the money appeared to be missing. As the day wore on into the late afternoon and my conversations among these people led to nothing, Holmes' absence began to concern me. It was well into the night before he made his return. Looking worse for wear with a pleased, smug look on his face, I was certain that he had returned to us knowing the truth behind this mystery. I was enjoying a spot of tea with Bradford when he made his entrance, just as we were beginning to wonder whether it would be appropriate to send out a search party.

"My dear Holmes, you look as though you have been

through the depths of the jungle. I thought that the tribe was only an hours trek from here. You have been gone for the better part of the day. Have you made any brilliant discoveries into the nature of this crime? I myself have come up empty I'm afraid."

"Watson, it appears that the answer to the motive behind this crime was the most obvious one from the beginning. Great wealth and fortune are hidden within these bushes. Now the only question is who will be willing to kill for it."

"Do you mean that on the journey to the Koburu you discovered that Sir Hughes was sitting on a great deal of wealth, and that someone was conspiring to take it from him?"

"Not Sir Hughes, my good man, but the tribe itself." As he said this, he pulled out from the sleeve of his shirt, a large amber colored gemstone; one that would be worth a great deal of money back home.

"I thought this was the safest place to keep it while trekking through the terrain, and there are a great deal more where this one came from. The tribal lands are sitting upon a field filled with these rare stones. Obviously, this was reason this case was so important to the higher ups of the British government, and surely, who ever knew about such a secret would have a great motive for murder."

My mind immediately turned to Bradford. With such an obvious motive, the last key to establishing his guilt was in place, and there he sat, with a look of complete innocence on his face. Though I didn't want to believe it, he had the motive as well as the opportunity.

"So tell me my friend, how long after Sir Hughes told you about this remarkable discovery, did you begin to plot his death? To sacrifice a great friend and a good man for a few gem stones. I had thought better of you than this."

As saying this, I raced inside my pocket to reach for my pistol unable to stop my thoughts from wondering to the worst conclusion. But I had, and there was nothing that he could say to make me believe different.

"Tell me, did you try to convince your dear friend to take the wealth and split it between the two of you, or did you plot to take the wealth for yourself from the beginning. Surely such a find would tempt even the strongest of men, but to murder a loyal friend over such a thing is beyond what I would have expected from you."

"Well", Holmes said, "it would seem that the final piece of the puzzle has fallen into place. The only problem is that I didn't know about this, and if I had, the moral and professional standards to which I hold myself would have forbidden me from even thinking such a thing. My career has been dedicated to the preservation of all people and their rights. To take these things that are so crucial to their lives and ceremonies would go against everything I have worked for my entire life. But I am afraid that you have jumped to the wrong conclusion in this case my dear Watson."

"It appears that he is correct, for the only person who would have the knowledge of these gems, as well as access to the scotch which was used to poison the victim, is none other than his loyal apprentice Gregory Rickman. Of course, when I made this discovery, and put the final pieces of the mystery together, Mr. Rickman had already made his escape."

"Escape, where could he have gotten too? There is no other way off of this island except by boat."

"That is correct Watson! And there just happens to be a supply boat preparing to leave the dock as we speak. If we make haste, we should get to them in time."

We quickly rushed to the dock that we had arrived on just three days before. We urged the boat to stop before they were too far away from the dock. As we boarded, we were assured by the crew members that there was no one else aboard, and that we should be looking elsewhere. They were persistent, but not overly so. Holmes, however, quickly surmised that the stowaway must be hiding beneath the deck. His hiding place was not great, although it can be assumed that Mr. Rickman had expected the handsome payment he had given to the members of the crew would afford him better protection than it had. For a small fee, the crew of the supply boat was willing to wait an hour or two as we returned the sack full of gems that were found on the stowaway and given back to the tribe. We gathered our belongings for the long voyage home. The journey back to the mainland was more uncomfortable than the one there with a smaller boat and more people aboard, but the relief of being off that sweltering island, more than made up for it. With our prisoner in hand, we made our way to England and back to the familiar comforts of home.

About the author

Pennie Mae Cartawick is an author of both fiction and nonfiction books. Her work is based on a variety of subjects including weight management and nutrition, recipe books, horror novelettes, and short Sherlock Holmes mysteries. She also draws her own illustrations for some of her short stories such as in "Silence Be Damned" and "The EXCHANGE". Her nonfiction books "Choosing the Right Diet for Success" and "The DETOX CLOCK" achieved the top 100 best seller list within the first week of publication.

She was born in the city of Sheffield in South Yorkshire England. Shortly after graduating high school, she worked as a Model and attended Shirecliffe College for Drama. Thereafter, she attended Stannington College for English, Art, communication skills and Photography. She then moved to London in her early 20's, where she studied and attained a career as a Beauty Therapist. She also obtained various certifications at DaneGlow International for slimming wraps and other deep heat treatments, and Thalgo Cosmetics for Makeup (a French Company focusing on Marine cosmetics). Her specialized skills include Makeup, Swedish massage, Reflexology, Nutrition, diet and exercise.

She Migrated to Florida in 1993 where she has been living

ever since. Although her profession Now-a-days is as a Real Estate Investor and a free-lance beauty consultant, her passion is writing, and uses the knowledge she acquired throughout the years on various subjects to enlighten others.

She is the youngest sibling of three, Anthony and Mark Cartawick.

Books

Choosing the Right Diet for Success

The DETOX CLOCK

7 Day Detox Smoothie Diet

THE FAST DIET

SILENCE BE DAMNED

The EXCHANGE

Ghost Stories

SHERLOCK HOLMES: The Mystery of the Faceless Bride

SHERLOCK HOLMES: The Mystery of the Poisoned Tomb

SHERLOCK HOLMES: A Strange Affair with the Woman on the Tracks

SHERLOCK HOLMES: The Case of the Cracked Mirror

SHERLOCK HOLMES: The Game of Cat and Mouse

SHERLOCK HOLMES: The Curse of a Native

SHERLOCK HOLMES: The Case of the missing Mayan Codices

SHERLOCK HOLMES: Murders on the Voyage to India

SHERLOCK HOLMES: The Sphinx Collection

SHERLOCK HOLMES: The Phoenix Collection

SHERLOCK HOLMES: The Ultimate Satyr Collection

SHERLOCK HOLMES: The Heist

SHERLOCK HOLMES: Death in the Tropics of an English Explorer

11372308R00113

Printed in Great Britain
by Amazon.co.uk, Ltd.,
Marston Gate.